GILA RIVER TRAILS

WESTERN SHORT STORY COLLECTION

DAN BALDWIN

GILA RIVER TRAILS
WESTERN SHORT STORY
COLLECTION

Published by Four Knights Press
www.fourknightspress.com
Cover Design and Layout Copyright © 2017
Based on original design by Aryn Livingston
Designed by Daring Creative Designs
daringcreativedesigns.com

ISBN-13: 978-1979206457
ISBN-10: 1979206457

OCTOBER 2017

GILA RIVER TRAILS

WESTERN SHORT STORY COLLECTION

TABLE OF CONTENTS

GILA RIVER TRAILS
WESTERN SHORT STORY COLLECTION

INTRODUCTION

A top-notch read, this is Dan's newest collection of short stories. Like a wedding, something old, new, borrowed and blue, TRAILS is a marriage of vignettes from his earlier works coupled with new tales of old Arizona. Each of the ten stand-alone stories captures scenes and moments and characters unique to Dan Baldwin's West. From the bawdy humor of GIRL FIGHT to the heart wrenching LETTERS FROM GIL CHESTERTON, each narrative is quick and colorful: sometimes raw, often poetic. To quote Coleridge, Dan uses "the best words in the best order." For followers of Dan's works, this is a must read. For newcomers, this is a great introduction to a unique and talented author.

—Micah S. Hackler, Author, Sheriff Lansing Mysteries

BLESSINGS FROM ABOVE

"**P**reacher needs a church." Caldera approached the town of Privy's patriarch with courage, but with some hesitation. The big man before him was just the deputy sheriff, but he was also one of the most powerful men in the territory.

Bull McKenzie doubled over and dry heaved. He tried to straighten up and made it about half way. "I need a shot of whiskey."

The younger man cleared his throat. "He ain't got no money and what the town gives him and that woman of his is barely enough to get by."

"Ain't my problem."

"Sure it is."

Bull reached for a small pouch in his vest, opened it and put some of the tobacco-like mass into his mouth.

Caldera said, "Is that moomsh?" A grin made a valiant, but failed effort to access his face.

Bull's eyelids clinched and he grunted an unintelligible, yet obviously vile answer.

Prospect, the big man's tormentor and only true friend, sat on the nearby porch. He laughed. "He is stove up again." Truly Bull's bowels had not been in the best of condition for a number of years. Moomsh, Pima for the Indian Wheat plant, was an excellent way to stimulate activity in the nether regions.

Bull said, "What's all this crap about Preacher's church? Don't he meet with them new townfolk back of the saloon?"

Prospect said, "A holy man should have a holy place."

Caldera said, "A church will keep him tied down – out of our hair, I mean."

Bull bent over slightly, his stomach beginning a familiar cramp. "Like I said, it ain't my problem."

Prospect said, "Preacher is your problem. He has been trying to convert your whores again."

"Good luck with—" Bull dry heaved.

"I bet them Easterners would like a real church," Caldera said.

"Don't you—" Bull's protest was cut off by a stomach cramp.

"It might even take up so much of Preacher's time he'd be too busy to pester your whores."

Bull grunted, "A... church... huh?"

"Think I'll run it by a couple of 'em. They're a cheap bunch though. I wonder who they'll start pestering for money and supplies."

"Bastard!"

Caldera grinned. "You ought to know, pop. Them Biblethumpers will still come pestering you. Unless the town he-bear...."

"Those Christers can build their own damn church."

Prospect, whose respect for holy men had grown through the years, had a brilliant thought. "No church, no more moomsh."

"I know plenty of Pima folk," Bull said.

It was Prospect's turn to grin. His wife was the best medicine woman in Arizona and the one who made the best moomsh.

"And pestering and pes-ter-ing," Caldera said.

"All right, damn it! Damn you both!"

So blackmail and constipation formed the foundation of the first Christian church in Privy, Arizona Territory. It was a good foundation. Bull, horrified at the thought of Easterners constantly dogging his trail, became a generous benefactor. He donated all of the major construction materials and even ordered Omar Whelming, chief engineer for his Bull's mining interests, to design the structure and oversee its construction. "Hell, man, if you can build a tunnel 1,000 feet underfoot, you can build a box for the Lord." He'd quickly learned that the world "Lord," with a capital L, moved some men when nothing else would. Banker Chandler, who constantly and proudly wore a waistband made from an old Confederate flag, donated lumber for pews, windows and doors, and the necessaries for making the interior presentable. The Easterners donated modest sums of money and enormous amounts of advice.

After Bull and Banker Chandler, the two largest donations came from surprising members of the community. Miss Rachael from the House of Doves brought in a sizeable amount of money collected by her employees. "We have but two modest requests. Any of my girls who wish to attend will attend."

Preacher didn't even hesitate. "Of course. All are welcome in the House of the Lord."

Miss Rachael took a deep breath and sighed. She had expected something of a moral struggle. Emboldened, she pressed on. "Some of my girls are Catholic."

Preacher spoke apologetically. "I don't have any denomination, Miss Rachael. I don't know anything about the Catholic Church and I surely don't speak Latin."

She nodded. "Perhaps you can acquire a Catholic Bible."

Preacher smiled. "Well, you can bet I'll try."

The need for Catholic services became obvious when a large contingent of the town's invisible community, the Mexicans, showed up to volunteer their labor. Chino Galleta, their spokesman, was also a master carver. As the walls went up and the roof put down, he invested a considerable amount of time working with wood and knife under a nearby cottonwood. When at last the windows were put in, the pews nailed tight, and the paint had dried, he presented Preacher with primitive, yet emotionally powerful carvings of the Fourteen Stations of the Cross.

Deanna Corley, Preacher's housekeeper, although not a Catholic, had been raised in large cities and had often attended services with friends. She took the carvings and, with Chino's help, placed them in proper position around the church. That settled it. There would be Protestant and Catholic services in Privy.

Not surprisingly, at least not to Bull, Caldera, Prospect, Miss Rachael and Chino, the Easterners pitched a fit. The matter of contention wasn't Catholicism. It was whores and Mexicans. The first church meeting held in the new building wasn't a service. It was a brawl. Such words as "harlot" and "peppergut" and "despicable" and "dirty" and "damnable" were thrown with fury equal to any Apache warrior with a lance and a hatred of someone moving in on his territory.

The matter was finally settled when Bull spoke. "All right, you bastards!" Mr. Gatling's gun could not have been more effective in silencing a mass of humanity. "Let's just tear the son of a bitch down." Banker Chandler stood up in a show of solidarity. He rested his thumbs in his Confederate flag, puffed his chest, and defied any one to speak against the motion. Miss Rachael and Chino, who had remained outside the church they had helped finance, nodded their assent.

Caldera, there to keep the peace in the Lord's house, saw a claw hammer next to a back wall. He grabbed it and immediately inserted the claw into the frame of a nearby window. "If we're gonna' do this, then let's get on with it." The loud creak of protesting wood that followed brought shouts of protest from the dissenters. Late in the evening a compromise was reached. Regular Sunday services would be held mid-morning till noon. The soiled doves would sit in the back pews. Services for the Catholic folks would be held one hour after dawn. The church would be open to functions for all with appropriate notice.

After the brawl and reconciliation a few men hung around to admire their work.

"All that shouting just to decide what you should'a known to do in the first place," Caldera said.

"We fought a bloody Civil War for the same reason," Omar Whelming said.

"I don't know what scared them more, Bull's threat or Mr. Chandler's big gut," Prospect said.

"It was the power of the Lord," Preacher said.

Caldera brandished his weapon. "And a good claw hammer."

They laughed a good bit over that and then stepped back to get a better view. The small square building stood alone at the edge of town. The moon had risen high and in the moonlight the church seemed to glow in the dark.

"I owe you, Caldera. This town owes you," Preacher said.

"It was just my idea. Them other folks did everything else."

"God bless you."

That was the first time in his life Caldera had ever heard that phrase tossed his way, but he gave it no thought. He looked at Preacher. "You seem a little down in the mouth."

"Oh, no. This is marvelous, a miracle. I was just thinking."

"Spit it out, Bub... ah, Preacher," Whelming said.

"Tomorrow's Sunday and our first real service."

"Yeah?"

"Oh, I just wish we had a steeple."

"Hell, Preacher - Sorry. We can build you one of those. Take a day or so," Whelming said.

"Fine... that's just fine," said Preacher, but they all could hear the disappointment in his voice.

The small group remained silent for a moment. Caldera cleared his voice. "I can get you a steeple for tomorrow morning."

"How!"

Caldera was reluctant to speak. "Why don't you go on home, Preacher? You just leave that steeple business to me, Prospect, an' Mr. Whelming."

After the parting, two confused men looked at Caldera. "What are you thinking?" Whelming said.

"We're wasting time. C'mon." Caldera dashed back toward town, quickly followed by two confused, tired and very interested men. Backhand Benny, watching from the nearest saloon, left a card game just forming and raced to join in. In less than a minute they had reached their destination, a small wooden structure next to the big wash behind the Armageddon Saloon. Caldera let fly with his idea. The others were for a second speechless.

"A privy for a steeple? You're out of your mind!" Whelming said.

"What do you think, Benny?" Caldera said.

"I can personally attest that it is functionally sound. Aesthetically, though...."

"Huh?"

"It'll work, but it stinks."

The small structure before them was a four by four square about six feet tall. The bottom half was made of rough horizontal planks. The top half was a crude lattice work topped by a peaked roof with four sides.

"We'd best get at it then," Caldera said.

The three men pulled their gloves up tight, pulled their neckerchiefs around their noses, and began the night's work. That task required some manhandling, a sled and horse, a hell of a lot of soap and water, and several coats of white paint. Whelming cut the bottom section with precision to match the slope of the roof. "The more of that bottom we cut off the better," Benny said.

The moment the paint was dry, which wasn't long in the arid climate, they disassembled the contraption, hauled it up to the church's roof and installed it properly at the appropriate location. A painted cross of two by fours topped the entire structure. Whelming even threw in some flashing to seal the edges. "We can make it pretty later. The main thing is Preacher will have his damn steeple for 'the good folk of Privy' tomorrow."

"It still stinks," Benny said.

"They won't notice it down there," Caldera said.

Preacher saw his new steeple during a glorious sunrise. He arrived just as the first rays of orange light struck the top of the cross and he marveled as the glowing light descended upon the new holy place. He said a short prayer of thanks for his blessings, mentioning Caldera by name.

Shortly after sunrise the Catholic whores and the Mexicans showed up for early morning services. They were grateful for the moment and the opportunity for real worship services in a real sanctuary. Preacher did his best at being a priest by talking a lot of Mary and love and overcoming adversity. He even spoke of the holiness of sacrifice and suffering. After the services the two groups dispersed quickly so as not to offend any of the other town folk who might come by the church early.

When the time arrived for regular services a good size crowd arrived with it. The women could only marvel at the appearance of a steeple atop the unadorned church they'd seen just the day before. Most of the men stifled their grins as best as possible. The general unspoken consensus was, "What the hell." The church needed a steeple and it got one. Just about everyone approved.

After services began, Bull and Prospect rode by, headed out for an afternoon of hunting. They both paused to stare at the overnight miracle. Privy's privy was now a church steeple.

When astonished, Prospect mingled his Pima and his English. "Biht house."

"Kind'a appropriate, ain't it?"

The two men laughed. The collective voices inside the church began singing as the two men rode away to the fading tune *of O'erwhelmed With Blessings From Above.*

(Adapted from *The Caldera Trilogy* by Dan Baldwin)

———◆———

GALL-GRRR

Jesus wandered the desert, fighting heat and cold, starvation, loneliness and loss and his own greatest fear: doubt. Moses before Him and scores of saints and addled would-be saints followed the same deadly road, but they struggled with a holy purpose toward a noble end even if that end meant death. O'Brien's wandering was far from holy or noble and his driving force was hatred. Another man's death would end the pilgrimage and then he would shuffle on. Some said revenge should be left to God, but a man has to believe in God to have that kind of patience.

His thoughts stuck to the man Gallager. *Stake him out. Gut him. Go fishing with his innards.*

Hunger clawed inside his belly, yet he stumbled past palo verde and mesquite trees without stopping. Their pods, a staple of desert dwellers' diet for thousands of years, rattled softly like diamondbacks in the wind. Thirst scratched his throat like sand across wounded flesh; no way could he eat. But when birds and wasps flew up a nearby ravine and the tracks of hundreds of small animals veered off the same way, he moved on.

Water.

He found only a dried mud hole. If animals laugh, Grat O'Brien was the source of much amusement that evening.

The larger, four-legged night hunters would have other thoughts.

His strong legs wobbled, but they carried him on. The downhill slope was gentle and the wash he followed twisted and turned like entrails cooking on a stick. Large rocks, tree stumps and fallen cactus created stumbling blocks for a man half-blind with sand and his own blood. He went around another bend and at last saw open space. He could see the plains between Bisbee and Tombstone. The pissant town of Pariah had to be down there too. He only had to stumble north and he would cross a road at some point. Some rider, a supply wagon, or a stage or cart hauling pilgrims to the new promise land would come along.

"Rescue my ass. Then Gal-grrr." He fainted.

***

Sometime later the shadows of a rocky outcrop to his left crossed his face. O'Brien jerked to awareness like a surprised animal. *Sundown.* He would never make it to the road in the dark. Hell, it was barely a scratch in the desert sand, so thin in some places he could stumble right over it and keep on wandering till he became pig scat.

He crawled up on all fours and found himself staring into the empty eye sockets of a human skull. It was skinless, hairless and bleached a pure white. *Been here a while, ain't ya?* The head probably belonged to a miner, cowhand or wandering mad man. O'Brien scanned the immediate area and spotted a small cave just above the wash. It had been carved out and expanded by human effort. *Miner.* The cave meant security and a safe place to spend the night, provided some mountain lion hadn't made a prior claim.

Although the slope was gentle, his climb up the short distance was an ordeal. Each stretch of his arm, each push of a leg, sent pointed shocks throughout his body. He had to get up there and out of sight. At that moment his mind had room for no other thought. Apaches were around and he couldn't risk being exposed. He was an easy target. The only thing that had saved him from death at the hands of the Indians earlier was the pitiful nature of the target. He was hardly trophy material. Still, some Apaches, especially the young braves out to prove themselves warriors, weren't known for their discrimination in selecting victims.

The mine was shallow and tapered off to a small hole into the mountain. There were no bones of mountain lion victims on the floor. He was safe. O'Brien crawled in and collapsed. The sun was down when his sixth sense kicked him awake. At the same time, that sense whispered *Don't move.* The weight on his back and a rapid buzzing sound tipped him off. *Rattlesnake!* As the evening temperatures cooled, the snake had crawled back into the cave where the rocks held in the heat of the day. O'Brien had crawled into a den of diamondbacks.

They came in slowly, one at a time, seeking the warmth of the cave and enjoying the unexpected comfort of a human body. Another snake took refuge on his butt as two others coiled up on each side, pinning his arms with the threat of certain pain and death. O'Brien took in a quick breath. The slight movement caused a terrifying buzz. He let it out slowly—oh, so slowly—and the buzzing stopped. He watched as the shadows grew longer, climbed uphill and swallowed the cave. The snakes snuggled closer.

In the westernmost part of the state at Yuma Prison, the guards often played a sick game with the inmates. The prisoners' cells featured a hole in the roof to allow circulation of the stink that passed for air. The guards dropped rattlesnakes and sometimes large scorpions through these holes at night and the inmates had to face a deadly enemy in total darkness. The slightest move brought a buzzing warning or in some cases a deadly strike. Men had been known to go insane during a single evening's entertainment. More than one had been killed by fear of a harmless king snake. O'Brien's situation was a lot worse. Any sudden move would bring on multiple strikes. A quick breath, a muscle spasm, stretching a muscle, yawning or any other movement could mean an agonizing and terrifying death. A single strike would cause a swift and natural reaction. He would move and then so would the snakes – a dozen or more at least.

O'Brien did not believe in God. He was only vaguely aware of the concept, but he prayed to something to keep him from sneezing. He could not afford the sleep he so desperately needed. His body begged for release, but his mind was aware enough to know the consequences. He would have to fight perhaps the greatest fight of his bitter, brawling life motionless. He allowed himself the luxury of blinking, but nothing more. Every once in a while a snake crawled in and out of his vision. For the most part, they remained behind, coiled up on or near him. He wanted to scream. At one point he was ready to shout, jump and make a foolish scramble down the hill.

But he would have doomed himself a second of the slightest movement. He would have been hit with multiple strikes to his legs and body, perhaps even his face. *An eye? My privates?* Blood and a small bit of saliva pooled in his mouth, but he feared even the slight movement of swallowing. He let the dark red goo dribble out the corners of his mouth.

At one point a large diamondback slithered across the floor of the cave and stopped directly in front of his face. Such was the force of his will that O'Brien did not even blink for several minutes. The snake moved away. As the gray light of false dawn brought out details in the desert below, he wondered how much longer he could survive under such conditions. Sleep meant death. Eventually sunlight struck the spines of a tall saguaro atop a nearby hill and the light hitting the spines gave it a descending halo as the sun climbed higher and higher. Small animals ran through the dust of the wash searching for food and the juicy plant leaves that carried the water for their survival. Slowly, seconds passing like minutes, the rattlers moved. One by one they crawled from the cave, seeking those same small creatures. Still, O'Brien did not move until he was sure he was the only living creature in that small cell.

His arms and legs were practically frozen in place from lack of movement. Sitting up was an act not only of courage, but of searing pain. He looked out the cave and into the desert and mountains. "Gallagher, I kill you slow." His words were a slurred growl, unrecognizable as speech. He half-scrambled, half-fell back down to the wash, and his long march began again. Distance wasn't the problem. He had to cover only a couple of miles. Time was his enemy. At best he had one day left in him and a day is a very small sliver of hope in such a wide desert.

He stumbled on. Down the mountain out there in the flatlands was the road and stages, shipping wagons, pilgrims, miners and ranchers: salvation. He did not know the word, but he knew its meaning and that thought kept him moving. He would need food soon, but water was an immediate need. No animal, not even Grat O'Brien, could survive long in the desert without it. He lacked the strength to even say the word.

The gods must have a sense of humor for they often grant a man that which his desires most, but the humor lies in the "how" more than in the "what." O'Brien swayed in the middle of the wash. A man of enormous strength, he could have been out fought and beaten by a ten year old. He fell to his knees and then onto all fours. He looked down to see a thin trickle of brown water running right beneath his head. Convinced it was a mirage, he smashed his fist into it. Dirty water splashed back in his face.

He looked back and saw that the stream was slightly wider. He bent down and sucked up a mouthful of mud. He used both hands to scoop out a small hole directly in the flow and within seconds it was full. He bent down again and this time drank real water. It stung his lips and his throat, but he drank again and again. The water was dirty and foul, but it meant life. To Gallager it meant death.

"Gall-a-ger...."

The narrow trickle of water touched both his knees and the flow was a half inch deep. Several birds took wing. Something rattled his brain and he heard a slight rumbling from back up the wash. He looked upstream and scrambled frantically toward the bank. The wash was alive in a flash flood. Somewhere up in the mountains the skies had rained like hell the previous night and now that hell was flowing his way. No wave of water rushed down on him. The wash turned to muck that seemed to rise up, slowly but powerfully, filling with sludge at a steady rate. By the time he got near the bank the water was pulling at his hips. The current carried large chunks of wood—entire tree trunks in some places—and large rocks rolled along the bottom of the wash.

He grabbed the low-hanging branch of a mesquite tree. It slipped out of his hand. A thigh-sized log smashed into his left hip and almost knocked him off balance. He fought and righted himself. A fall into those waters would take him under to be ground to a pulp. The bank was giving way. He pulled harder, grabbed the narrow tree trunk and pulled himself onto the bank. As it caved in he scrambled farther and found his way to safety.

The entire flood was over in less than half an hour. He drank deeply from water trapped in a *tinaja*, a natural hole in a rock in the bed of the wash. There would be more all the way to the base of the mountain.

He would find the road and return to Pariah. And, like Jesus, Gallager would spend a night in the desert – in a cave. Unlike Jesus, Gallager would not live 40 days.

(Adapted from *Trapp Canyon* by Dan Baldwin)

THE FILE ON JOHN RINGO

Memo
TO: *Sheriff Bodie*
FROM: *Deputy Stroud*
RE: *John "Johnny" Ringo File*

I have reviewed the original reports, contemporaneous accounts, articles, stories and other materials (some of dubious value) relating to the John Peters "Johnny" Ringo file. A sampling of the materials I have studied is attached for your review. Note that some of the material is at best ludicrous while other materials are of legitimate value. Samples of each are included simply to demonstrate the kind of crap you have put me through.

L.E. Stroud

(You owe me more than one beer.)

# # #

Knowing that God and right were on my side, I called out the miscreant Ringo. My voice thundered with righteous wrath. "Miscreant! If you dare, confront a man face-to-face, a man who fears neither you nor death, but only dishonor. Come forth!"

The Ringo Kid hid behind the boulder that would soon become his bloodied tombstone. Shaking, he bit his leathered lower lip. His hand, slippery with drops of fear, clasped the weapon that had lead-bludgeoned the life of many a good man. He was a cur of monstrous proportions.

I shouted again. "Justice is calling your name. It shouts 'coward!"

At that moment the Kid jumped from behind his granite sanctuary, guns blazing Hell's own fury. I fired but once. The bullet, guided by God's grace and a good aim, found its home in the man's breast where no Christian heart ever beat, for the man was truly heartless.

"Is he dead," someone asked.

"Yes, for I have killed him."

"You killed the Ringo Kid!"

"Yes, I have killed the Ringo Kid."

"Ringo dead."

"Yes, dead is Ringo."

(From *The Cowardly Death of Johnny Ringo and the Revenge of Justice Prevailing* by Luther Foote, self-published 1897)

Note to Sheriff Bodie: this is what I mean by "crap."

# # #

"I had stopped off at the Smith place to pass a few moments with old friends. We were enjoying coffee and cigars when we heard the shot. We didn't think nothing of it at the time. The odd shot along Turkey Creek is fairly common – hunters mostly, drunks sometimes. I spent the night and it wasn't until after sunrise we noticed John Ringo... turned out it was his body... against a tree. We ran over and I could tell right away that something was way the hell wrong. First thing was his head and the way his...."

(From the Diary of J.W. Armstrong – the page is torn away at this point and no relevant information was recorded in the surviving pages.)

# # #

Turkey or Morse's Hill Creek
14ᵗʰ July, 1882
Statement for the information of the Coroner and Sheriff of Cochise Co. A.T.

There was found by the undersigned John Yoast the body of a man in a clump of Oak trees about 20 yards north from the road leading to Morse's mill and about a quarter of a mile west of the house of B.F. Smith The undersigned viewed the body and found it in a sitting posture, facing west, the head inclined to the right—There was a bullet hole in the right temple, the bullet coming out on top of the head on the left side. There is apparently a part of the scalp done including a small portion of the forehead and part of the hair, this looks as if cut out by a knife. (These are the only marks of violence visible on the body.) Several of the undersigned identify the body as that of John Ringo, well known in Tombstone. He was dressed in light hat, blue shirt, vest, pants and drawers, on his feet were a pair of hose and undershirt torn up so as to protect his feet. He had evidently travelled but a short distance in this foot gear. His revolver he grasped in his right hand, his rifle rested against the tree close to him. He had on two cartridge belts, the belt for the revolver cartridges being buckled on the upside down....

The body of the deceased was buried close to where it was found. When found deceased had been dead about 24 hours.

Thomas White	James Morgan
John Blake	Robert Boller
John W. Bradfield	Frank McKinney
B.F. Smith	W. J. Darnal
W.W. Smith	J.C. McGrager
A.E. Lewis	John Yoast
A.S. Neighbors	Fred Ward

"ENDORSED"
Statement by citizens in regard the death of
John Ringo
Filed Nov. 12/82
W. H. Seamans, Clk.
By Louis A. Souc, Depy.
(The Official Coroner's Report on John Peters Ringo)

# # #

The somewhat contradictory reports on the demise of one Johnny Ringo leave us with a mystery. The suicide theory is backed by eyewitnesses who report that the man had become despondent in 1882, perhaps because of a rejection by his family when he paid them a visit in San Jose. Other witnesses report that his drinking, significant to say the least, had increased and that he was barely conscious due to heavy drink when seen the evening of his death. Others speculate murder.

(J. T. Spaulding, Live History Online podcast, July 14, 2010)

# # #

"Suicide? There's no way, young man. Remember, I was there. I talked to some of the men on that coroner's jury. You tell me a man who's gonna do hisself in is gonna scalp hisself first. Bah! And that hat. How the...H--- are you gonna blow your brains out, but leave your hat still on your head? You tell me that, young man?"

(Don Simmons, From Radio Recollections, CBS Radio Network, 1934)

# # #

"The Earps did it, I tell you."

"Hell, no, Sam. It was Johnny Behind the Duce. He hated Ringo."

"My money's on Leslie."

(Conversation recorded for History TV's documentary Old Timers of Tombstone

# # #

RINGO MASSACRED... REQUEST ARREST AND HOLD OF EARP AND HALLIDAY (sic). RESPOND IMMEDIATELY. SHERIFF, COCHISE COUNTY, A.T.

(Telegram found in possession of Mrs. Mildred Hyde of Bisbee, AZ. The document is disputed as a fake.)

# # #

DEATH OF JOHN RINGO

His Body Found in Morse' Canyon

Sunday evening intelligence reached this city of the finding of the dead body of John Ringo near the south of Morse's Canyon in the Chiricahua Mountains on Friday afternoon. There was few men in Cochise country, or southeastern Arizona better known. He was recognized by friends and foes as a recklessly brave man, who would go any distance or undergo any hardship to serve a friend or punish an enemy. While undoubtedly reckless, he was far from being a desperado, and we know of no murder being laid in his charge. Friends and foes are unanimous in the opinion that he was strictly honorable man in all his dealings, and that his word was as good as his bond.

(The Tombstone Epitaph, July, 1882)

# # #

RINGO DEAD
Murderous Career At An End At Last
Community Rejoices End of Terror
(Headline, The Bisbee Bee, July, 1882)

# # #

RINGO DEAD
Another Bright Light Snuffed Out
Community Mourns Grave Loss of Leading Citizen
(Headline, The Bisbee Banner, July, 1882)

# # #

Sheriff Bodie – Perhaps the most cogent account of what could have happened and what probably did happen is found in this ASU "Recording Our History" program, taped sometime back in the forties. The subject of the interview, Dwight Hullbertson, was a colorful local history buff who actually met Ringo when he – Hulbertson – was a kid. I transcribed a bit of it.

INTERVIEWER: What was meeting Johnny Ringo like?

HULLBERTSON: First off, sonny boy, didn't nobody call him "Johnny." At least not to his face. He hated that name.

INTERVEWER: Do you think Wyatt Earp killed Ringo?

HULLBERTSON: Hell no. Can I say that?"

INTERVIEWER: It's your interview, Mr. Hullbertson.

HULLBERTSON: Wyatt and that Holliday friend of his were in Colorado when they got Ringo. It's documented. And John O'Roarke, Johnny-Behind-The-Duce they called him, didn't do it either. He left Arizona a year 'for the shooting.

INTERVIEWER: You said "they" got Ringo. Who do you mean?

HULLBERTSON: Who the hell do you think! Old Buckskin Frank Leslie and Billy Claiborne. They be the ones who killed Ringo. Hell, everybody knew it. Especially after Frank dropped the Kid. That was right outside the Oriental. I was coming out of the Grand Hotel where I had a little job helping clean—

INTERVIWER: Back to the Ringo killing, please.

HULLBERTSON: Yeah. You know the trouble with these so-called experts? They never go to the scene of the crime. You go out there today. It's 'bout like it was back then. You go out there and in one look you can tell exactly what happened. Old John, so drunk he couldn't pour whiskey in a barrel with the end knocked out, sat down against that tree – probably passed out. They most likely were following him for some time and this was their chance. I think they crawled up Turkey Creek, got a good bead on John and fired off a round right through his head. They rushed up and did all the rest – the gun belt, the cutting on his head, moving his boots and all that – they did that just to confuse things. It worked, too.

INTERVIEWER: You're sure about Leslie and Claiborne?

HULLBERTSON: You know what Billy Claiborne's last words were, sonny?

INTERVIEWER: No, sir.

HULLBERTSON: He said, and I know it for a fact, he said "Frank Leslie killed John Ringo. I saw him do it." That's his exact words. If I'm lying I'm dying."

# # #

...Frank Leslie was to go with us and may yet, if he is not detained in killing matter of this morning, and he ought not to be. He shot and killed the notorious Kid Claiborne this A.M. at 7:30, making as pretty a center shot on the Kid as one could wish to.

The Kid threatened and laid for him near the Oriental with a Winchester, but Frank got the drop on him, being quick as lightning and used to killing men, and the Kid has gone to Hell."

(From the Diary of George Whitwill Parsons)

# # #

The most telling to me, Sheriff, and the one bit of information we can never use in a court of law comes from a couple of psychics – don't snarl – over in Huachuca City. They say they "chat" with Ringo at the grave site and have even recorded his voice. It's something they call EVPs or electronic voice phenomena. I include it just because it's interesting and in a way it kinda' give John Ringo the last word on all this. Their names are Don and Rolanda. And I swear, boss, that voice on the tape is not either one of them.

# # #

DON: Session Two. Ten-Fourteen a.m. Rolanda and I have moved to the John Ringo actual gravesite.

(Some material deleted here, Sheriff)

ROLANDA: Do you know who shot you, John?

EVP: (very faint but audible) Yes.

DON: Was it Leslie? Buckskin Frank Leslie?

(ten second pause)

Did you hear anything?

ROLANDA: No. Not a thing.

DON: Was it Billy Claiborne?

ROLANDA: Nothing.

DON: I don't think he wants to talk to us now.

ROLANDA: I'm picking up that he just wants to be left alone.

DON: Yeah. I get that.

ROLANDA: There's a lot of controversy about how you died, John... Mr. Ringo. Is there anything, anything at all you'd like to say before we go?

EVP: F*** it!

# # #

Like they say, Sheriff, where there's smoke there's fire. It is my opinion that the "cold case" should be reclassified from suicide to undetermined. From what I've come across we have a fire on our hands. Do we want to fan it or just hope that it burns out?

Now, about those beers....

Readers interested in learning more about historical/paranormal work about the death of John Ringo should read *Speaking with the Spirits of the Old Southwest - Conversations with Miners, Outlaws, and Pioneers Who Still Roam Ghost Towns* by Dan Baldwin and Dwight and Rhonda

Hull available from Lewellyn Worldwide in ebook and paperback May, 2018.

Rocks Move

"**R**ocks move." If a broken clock can be right two times a day, then a mind-numbed brute like Grat O'Brien might occasionally recognize his ass from a hole in the ground. He leaned forward facing a wall of shattered rock, spread eagle to keep the piss from running down his leg. O'Brien urinated like a mule, what little thought processes he focused on the steady stream falling to the earth. For 30 or 40 seconds that stinking waterfall was his entire universe. A slight crack in the dark stone wall slipped left a half-inch or so, then zipped back the opposite direction before settling in its original position, making a slight grinding noise. Earthquakes are common in Arizona and so mild as to be ignored, a dangerous and deadly way of thinking when a man is 100 feet into a tunnel 40 feet below the desert.

"Rocks move."

"Yeah, rocks move, you damn idjit. We hit rocks. We pick up rocks. We chunk rocks. Rocks move. That's what miners do." Browny Powell struck his pick against the milky-white crystal vein they were following. It shattered, revealing tiny streaks of silver, the glint of someone else's fortune. He struck again, even harder.

"Get back to work, dumbass," Ty Munroe said. During the past months they had discovered just enough silver to keep the mine running, the owners encouraged, and the three miners in beans, bread and booze.

O'Brien buttoned up his britches, grabbed his shovel and threw more rubble into the loading cart. "Rocks still move."

Munroe stopped hammering and rubbed his nose. "Jeeze, O'Brien! This ain't no piss pot. Next time you gotta' take your snake for a walk, go down to the shaft where there's a little air."

"How the hell did you get miners work," Powell said.

"I'm strong."

"With all them muscles in your head I guess so," Powell said.

Munroe tossed a rock at O'Brien. It struck the lantern on his head, knocking the candle out and to the ground. He fumbled around with lighting and stuck it back in his hat.

"Idjit."

"Dumber'n a bucket of bolts."

O'Brien dropped his shovel and doubled his fists.

Munroe's attitude changed significantly by the time the shovel's handle hit the hard rock. *Stupid bastard'll kill me.* "Just funning, O'Brien. I didn't mean nothing by it." Munroe shifted the pick in his hand, making it a weapon. He had seen O'Brien's rage and the damage he could do to another man. "Let's get back to work. We got to earn some fat sumbitch over in Tombstone another big house on the hill."

O'Brien placed his hand against the wall. "Rocks move again."

"You dumb Son of a—"

A loud, deep boom rumbled through the mine, like thunder or an explosion. The earth trembled. Dust, like a light brown mist, floated from the ceiling to mix with the disturbed earth bouncing on the floor. It blurred the dim light like a cloud suddenly passing before the sun.

"What the hell? Did somebody blow up the shack?" Powell said. He knew better. The explosion came from within the earth, not from the storage shed above. He looked down the tunnel. It was swaying back and forth like a rope bridge across a steep gorge. A small rain of rock from the roof followed the dust. The sound was like hail on a hardwood surface. "Christ! We gotta' get out of here!"

"Run!" Munroe's scream was hoarse and guttural, almost primeval.

O'Brien was slow to move. Munroe tripped over him. Powell scrambled over the human obstacles and crawled toward the shaft. The tunnel cracked. Large chunks of rock fell the entire length and a dust storm rolled over and blinded the men. The noise was overwhelming. Another explosion caused Powell to shriek. Munroe curled up in a fetal position, trying to protect as much of his body as possible. O'Brien swatted at the dust so he could see. Falling rock fell on fallen rock and the bright beam of light from the shaft slowly became a sliver, and then a tiny, dim glow. It appeared to be falling away from them.

In less than a minute the quake was over. No one spoke for some time. Powell at last gasped as if he had been holding his breath through the entire ordeal. "Cave in."

"Rocks move."

"Why didn't you say something, you damn moron?" Powell said.

"He did, shit fer' brains. We was dumber than the dumbass."

"He done killed us."

"Shut up."

Powell sat down and put his head between his knees. "We're dead men." He whimpered.

Munroe stared at the wall of debris between them and their only possibility of escape. The fallen rock had to extend most if not all the way to the vertical shaft. He turned on O'Brien, his voice full of anger, desperation and fear. "You should have made us listen, idjit! This is your fault!" He stuck his face to the small crack at the top of the rubble. He could see light from the shaft. "At least we won't suffocate."

Powell said, "I hate to think my last breath's gonna be the smell of O'Brien's piss."

O'Brien grabbed the man by his shirt and tossed him to the floor. He looked through the narrow shaft to the light. "I get us out."

"How?" Munroe said.

"Move rocks."

"Hell, man, some of them boulders weigh a couple of hundred pounds."

"I can move 'em."

Powell looked up, his face showing fear and hope. One look at O'Brien's emotionless face brought out more whimpering. "Hell, he even smells dumb."

"Me 'n Powell can move around them smaller stones. You really think you can move the big ones? Dig us a crawl space outta' here?"

O'Brien turned and began tossing the smaller rocks to the back of the mine, freeing up access to the first large boulder. One of the rocks struck Powell in the head.

"Careful, you oaf!" Powell picked up a stone and threw it at O'Brien's back.

Munroe's arm shot out and the rock bounced off his hand. "Get up here and help us."

Powell buried his head farther into his arms and knees. "We're dead men."

O'Brien grabbed him, picked him up and threw him against the wall. "Move rocks!"

Munroe helped Powell up and they cleared rocks away from the first boulder. Like most of the rest down the tunnel, they could have been moved by two or three men with modest effort. O'Brien didn't think about the odds. He just moved. The confined space of the mine barely allowed one man access, and Grat O'Brien was a very big man. He squeezed himself in between the boulder and the tunnel wall. He worked his way around by tossing out more of the smaller rocks. When he couldn't bend over, he kicked with his feet and toes.

Munroe laughed. He examined a crystal O'Brien had tossed out. A solid line of pure silver ran along one edge. "Jeeze, that damn quake found us a big vein. Our buryin' clothes is gonna be a coat of silver."

O'Brien, unthinking, just kept working. He pushed against the boulder with his arms.

Munroe and Powell did what little they could to pull from the other side. The rock moved enough for O'Brien to work his way behind it. He used his feet and the strength in his legs to push. The rocks at his back cut through his clothes and into his skin. Within moments the boulder rolled away and Munroe and Powell danced out of the way. They looked back to see more rocks and more boulders.

"It don't stop," Powell said.

O'Brien didn't waste a second. He just started in on the next pile of rubble, always doing the labor of two or three men. He had only two choices: move or die. He never gave much thought to life or living—he just stumbled from one lousy mistake to another—but he definitely did not want to die. The fire within, the will to overcome and deny death, was strong. Although he rarely used his mind to think beyond his immediate wants, his body didn't need thoughts or plans to escape this trap. He moved rock and shoved boulders. His back was ripped and cut so badly that many of the boulders handled by Powell and Munroe were streaked with red. He pushed on, oblivious to the pain.

They stopped at nightfall when proceeding further represented a greater danger than resting. The food and water they craved was nearby, but on the other side of the cave in and 40 feet up a wooden ladder. O'Brien, who had done the heaviest and most dangerous work, never complained. Powell was breaking and Munroe was nearing his own breaking point.

"You should have warned us, you moron!" Powell threw a rock at the next big boulder blocking their escape. 'Rocks move.' What the hell kind of warning is that! Rocks move. Damn, fool."

"Shut up, Powell. He can't help it he's a mutton head. Ain't that right, Mutton head?"

O'Brien's only response was a snore.

"Idjit."

"That idjit might just dig us outta this crap," Munroe said.

"Well, I ain't working with him no more. No sir."

"I'll talk with Hayden. Say it's all O'Brien's fault."

"Fire his ass, f'shur."

"He won't be working around these parts no more."

"The oaf."

Neither man noticed that O'Brien was no longer snoring.

The sound of rocks hitting the ground at their feet woke Munroe and Powell. The faintest of lights showed in the narrow space between the new ceiling and the rubble below. O'Brien was working at a more furious pace than he had the day before. The two men joined in without a word. And that is how the second day passed. O'Brien threw rocks or rolled them across the floor of the mine. Munroe and Powell piled them out of the way. They were animals functioning in a system requiring neither communication nor command.

The air was foul enough to make most men sick. Powell and Munroe were on their last legs and they moved like men half-alive. Conversation was limited to the occasional cussword or reference to O'Brien's ignorance. Powell passed out three times, the last a pitiful effort to let the others carry on his share of the work. Munroe wasn't fooled and O'Brien, if he cared at all, did not show it. Munroe forced his co-worker back on the job with a curse, a threat and a kick to his butt. A death stare from O'Brien closed the sale and Powell crawled back to work.

O'Brien kicked them into action the morning of the third day.

"It ain't no use," Powell said.

"Give it up, O'Brien," Munroe said.

"The rocks move us, now we move rocks," O'Brien said.

"You're simple. Can't you see it's over?" Powell said.

O'Brien said nothing. He just tossed more rocks from their roadblock. Powell and Munroe dodged them for a while and finally stood up and staggered to work. They were exhausted. O'Brien seemed as strong as ever. He was certainly as determined as ever. He moved slowly, but powerfully and rock by rock he cleared a path.

"It's shining!" Munroe said. Light filtering in through the shaft filled the dusty trap with a soft, almost golden glow. Dust particles spiraled down, dancing in the spotlight.

Powell grinned. "He did it! The moron did it!"

O'Brien shoved the last large boulder back and stepped into a shaft of light. Munroe and Powell crawled through like spiders. The sunlight was bright and almost directly overhead.

Powell, his face down, scrambled for the meager supply of food and water they had left three days earlier. He saw only rubble. "Damn."

"Oh hell," Munroe said. He was looking up.

Forty feet of rough-hewn wood that had been their ladder, their lifeline to the surface, lay at their feet in a pile of splintered and shattered beams.

"Firewood. Let's just build a damn fire and float up on the smoke," Powell said. He sat down and resumed his standard posture with his head between his knees.

Munroe stared upward. "No way we can rebuild that ladder."

"God." Powell's words were mixed with his standard whimpering. He grabbed a handful of pebbles and threw them at O'Brien's feet. The big man ignored the insult.

"Faulk," O'Brien said.

Powell sat up, his spirits buoyed. "The supply wagon!"

Munroe picked up a fragment of the ladder and tapped it against the wall of their cage. "Faulk's coming. Today... three days... maybe next week some time." He slammed the stick against the wall and let it bounce to the ground.

"He's gotta' get here today, Munroe."

"If he don't get drunk. Or shack up with that whore of his. If the Apaches don't get him."

Powell sank back. "I can't do it, Munroe. I won't make it."

O'Brien examined the shaft. They were trapped in a four by four foot hole. The walls were rough, but straight.

Munroe sat down, picked up another wooden fragment and tapped it against the floor. "Three days without food or water. We're flat worn out. Hell, I give us a fifty-fifty chance if Faulk don't get here in three days. Two's pushing it."

"Climb," O'Brien said.

Powell threw a small rock at O'Brien. "You are a moron! You expect us to just walk up them walls like that staircase in the Birdcage? Maybe some pretty little hostess will serve us whiskey and beer on the way up. She might even hike her skirt and let us take one from shooter's hill! Christ."

O'Brien doubled his fists and just as quickly relaxed. The walls were closing in on him too. He looked up. Clean air was up there. Food and water, and some booze was in a shack just forty feet away. Forty feet. "I'll climb."

"You really think you can get up those walls?" said Munroe.

"I'm strong."

"What the hell? If the muscles in your arms and legs are as strong as the one in your head, you just might make it," Munroe said.

"I can make it."

"Hell, man. Get going."

"Tired."

"Rest when you get up there."

Munroe gave him a boost with his hands. O'Brien grabbed a small outcropping with his right hand and pulled up. He grabbed another with his left hand, pulled again and sought a foot hold. He dangled and kicked, but finally found a small spot for the edge of his boot sole. He reached and pulled and struggled for foot holds again and again. His fingertips bled. His shoulders ached and the muscles knotted into cords of tight pain. He was so close to the rock his face bled from scratches and cuts. *Reach. Pull. Reach. Step. Pull. Pull. Pull.*

"Can't." He gasped and reached up only to fall. The drop was almost fifteen feet, but he landed on his legs. He stumbled and fell, but he didn't break any bones.

Try again, moron!" Powell said in a high-pitched shriek.

Munroe pushed him down and turned his attention to O'Brien. "You've been doing this all wrong."

"You climb."

"I can't. I got nothing left. You gotta' do this. Otherwise they may as well just cover us up and say some fancy words."

"My arms don't work."

"Listen to me. Use those big legs of yours to push yourself up. Don't use your arms for anything but hanging on. Let your legs do the work."

"Legs do the work."

"You ain't the brightest lamp in the bunkhouse, O'Brien, but you can do this. Remember, climb with your legs and just hang on with your arms. You can remember that can't you?"

"Yeah."

"I'll give you a boost."

O'Brien climbed again. He clung to the rocks with his hands, struggled to find any foothold possible and pushed himself up farther. He climbed. He slipped several times, but did not fall. His fingers cramped and stiffened, locked into position, yet he forced them to grab and hold. He took out his anger on the rock. "Can't... kill... me... bitch!"

Munroe stood below him. A beat of sweat dropped twenty or so feet onto his face. He wiped it away. It was tinted red with blood. He stepped back.

O'Brien struggled no more than 20 or 30 minutes, but to the three men his ordeal seemed to take hours. When he threw a leg over the edge and crawled away, Powell cried. Munroe sat back and breathed out a burst of air. He and Powell looked at each other and broke out laughing, releasing three days of fear and tension in a few seconds of lost control. "The idjit did it!" Powell said. They celebrated as if the victory over death was theirs alone.

On the surface O'Brien rolled over and caught his breath. His arms were afire, his legs wobbly and his fingers frozen in place, like the claws of a dead bird of prey. He pushed them against the hot sand to force them into position so he could use them. He gasped and breathed deeply. He had pushed himself almost beyond human limits, struggling on when others would have given in to defeat and a slow death. His efforts were a marvel of human endurance. He had not even caught his breath when the shouts started from below.

"Throw us a rope, moron!"

"Get us out of here!"

O'Brien walked over to the supply shed and measured out the appropriate length of rope. He coiled it and walked to the edge of the mine. "You want rope?"

"Throw it down here, idjit!"

"O'Brien!" His name was a command.

"You want rope?"

"Yes, damn it!"

"Yours." O'Brien threw the entire coil down the hole. He walked away from their curses and sat down in the shade of the shed. He reached up and took a bottle of whiskey, their last, from its shelf and drank deeply. Some men enjoy a shot of whiskey, even bad whiskey. They appreciate the slow burn down the gullet and the pleasing after-effect. O'Brien drank because he liked that kick in head. He often kicked himself in the head till he was unconscious.

Below, the curses turned into demands, and the demands became pleas. When they began begging he coiled up another length of rope. He finished the whiskey and, as dehydrated as he was, it produced the desired effect; O'Brien was drunk. He jammed an iron bar into the ground at an angle away from the mine and pounded it almost all the way in with a sledgehammer before tying off the rope. He tossed the rope down and towered over the square hole in the ground.

"O'Brien dumb?"

"No! Sharp as a tack!"

"Smart as a whip!"

Powell grabbed the lifeline. There was no room for flipping a coin in his mind. He struggled up and O'Brien pulled him out. Powell dusted himself off and walked straight to the shed. He returned holding the empty whiskey bottle. "You drank it all, you addled-brain mor—"

O'Brien struck and pulled back his fist as Powell slammed to the earth, his jaw broken. He got up on all fours, but O'Brien kicked him in the gut. Powell saw two of everything and his head felt like it was expanding and contracting with every beat of his heart. He nearly retched as O'Brien picked him up and threw him into a patch of cholla cactus. Hundreds of sharp spines, each one with a tiny hook on the end, skewered his flesh. He screamed and rolled away. Hundreds of more spines found a home in his skin. O'Brien's shadow covered him, and Powell smelled a foul odor as he soiled himself.

"Who's the moron now?"

O'Brien picked up a small boulder, probably weighing ten or fifteen pounds, and heaved it into Powell's gut. The man screamed. He rolled away and more cactus spines worked their way into his flesh. Screaming, he scrambled out of the cactus and dry heaved. His body was so covered with cactus spines he couldn't lie down. He rested on all fours and heaved again.

Munroe struggled to pull himself out of the mine. "What the hell's going on?" His hands scratched at the dirt and rock as he worked forward on his elbows to bring the rest of his body all the way out. His foot slipped and he fell back a few inches. Panic widened his eyes. *No! Not this way!* O'Brien walked over and pulled him out. "I won't hurt you so much, Munroe." Before Munroe could say, "What the hell?" O'Brien smashed his fist into the man's stomach. He doubled over only to meet an uppercut that knocked him on his butt.

Munroe didn't move.

Powell whined, but he said nothing.

"Not so dumb now?" O'Brien walked back to the shed and threw a saddle on their mule, the only means of transportation available. He rode over to Munroe and pointed west toward Tombstone. "Go that way. Don't follow me."

"No sir." Munroe watched until O'Brien was out of sight, headed east, before he stood up. Powell wept. The pain was too intense. Munroe limped to the shed and dug out a pair of leather gloves and a pair of pliers. Powell's screaming stopped about mid-afternoon, replaced by a pitiful sobbing. Munroe said nothing. He just kept pulling cactus spines from the man's body. *To hell with this. I'm going back to the States.*

The rocks moved one more time – just a rumble, but enough to cave in one side of the mine. The two beaten and busted men looked at each other, stood up and moved on down the road.

Only the Best
for Mister Abaddon

"**O**nly the best, Mr. Davis, only the best. I may not have much, but all that I own is nothing but the best."

"Looks like quite a spread to me, Mr. Abaddon." Lewton Davis, gunman for hire, looked around the hacienda's interior court. The wealth and luxury on display contrasted sharply with the dull façade of the thick, whitewashed adobe walls surrounding the small fortress. A central fountain bubbled with fresh water from some spring deep in the bowels of the earth. The bubbling sounding like anxious whispers from some nearby dark room. Carefully placed and well-tended mesquite trees provided small oases of spotty shaded. The courtyard was large enough to allow in gusts of wind which blew up swirling circles of sand as if the dirt was trying to flee upwards for escape. Each wall was lined with small sheds, workshops apparently. Most of them were occupied by men or women practicing their solitary craft.

Abaddon, an agreeable looking, portly, man in his early fifties placed both fists on his hips and surveyed his kingdom.

Davis jabbed the sharp toe of his boot into the ground and kicked sand over one of the many scorpions crawling toward his shadow. "About that job, Mr. Abaddon...."

"In time, my boy, in time. Please indulge me as I show you my... museum. A tour will help you understand the nature of your task. Come." He led Davis to the first of many stalls or sheds and pointed to an old man carving a crucifix. The walls were lined with them, each one upside down with bright red paint dripping into small tin buckets. Abaddon leaned over to inspect the man's work. "I got Sanchez here in Santa Fe. He is the finest sculptor in wood on the continent. At one time you could find his work in the finest cathedrals on two continents."

Davis feigned interest.

Abaddon snapped his fingers. "He's mine now."

The next shed sheltered a woman, a Navajo by the looks of her. She was weaving a red and black rug of substantial size. "This is Doli. Her name means blue bird." Abaddon reached to the far wall and thumped a birdcage lightly. A blue bird within fluttered slightly. "I keep this creature so she will have her namesake as company." Doli kept to her weaving and never looked up. "She is the greatest artist in weaving in the entire Navajo Nation. Many braves have offered gold, even horses to win her hand."

"And you won out. Over braves?"

"I see, my boy, that you are incredulous. Ha! Believe me, even a civilized, rotund fellow like myself has more to offer a woman than an adobe Hogan in the desert. Her invaluable services cost me little more than a herd of sheep to a desperate father. Come, I have more to show you."

Abaddon's menagerie included a bootmaker of incredible skill; a metalworker forging glowing wonders in gold, silver and brass; and a gardener whose skill was evident in the luxurious growth within the compound. The grand tour was incomplete and only lasted ten minutes or so. He led Davis inside the hacienda. The floor was a dark tile. The white walls were covered in exquisite tapestries and an incredible number and variety of fine paintings.

Davis said, "You don't have to be no art critic to see you know your stuff, sir."

"As I said, Mr. Davis—

"Just Davis."

"Ah... as I said, I am obsessed with acquiring the best – the best of everything. And I want you to assist with my next acquisition."

"Uh, what would that be, Mr. Abaddon?"

"A man, Davis, the very best in his... line of work. Come."

He guided Davis through the main room and down a hall to a locked door. Once inside, Abaddon lit a lamp and led Davis down a flight of stairs and through another locked door. The room was as luxuriously appointed as the rest of the hacienda. It was dominated by a small number of stuffed beasts: a lion, a Kodiak bear, and a great bald eagle. Each was mounted on a highly polished, dark wooden stand inset with a brass plate noting the creature's species and the time and date of capture. A fourth block held a large glass container with a heavy lid. A brass plate was next to it.

"Wine, Davis?"

"Whiskey if you got it."

"A man who, as they say, likes fire in his belly. I like that, my boy, I like that."

"Yeah. Meanin' no disrespect, Mr. Abaddon, can we move—"

"Patience is a virtue, my boy. Impatience will get you killed."

"I got word that you're looking for a man who can do a certain kind of work. I'm that certain kind of man, sir. And I'd like to get on with it if we can."

Abaddon's eyelids narrowed, but his smile never wavered. He pour two fingers of very dark whiskey from a crystal decanter. "Scotch Whiskey, Davis. I doubt that you have had the privilege."

"Whiskey's whiskey." Davis took the glass. He sniffed the liquor. His lips formed a slight sneer. He sipped it and then finished the drink in a single swallow."

Abaddon smiled broadly. "An acquired taste."

"Uh-huh. I'll take another snort if you don't mind."

"I see you have an affinity for the best also."

"I don't know what no affinity is, but if I got to wait for you to get to the point...."

"To get down to business, eh?"

"Yes, sir."

"I noticed you noticing my menagerie?

"Your what?"

"The beasts. My collection. They, too, represent the best. They rule the land we walk upon and the air we breathe." He paused and flicked a finger toward the empty blocks. "Next year I will enter the Pacific Ocean to bring back a great white shark – a killer unmatched in any ocean."

"That other block? The one with the glass jar on it?"

Abaddon poured another large shot of whiskey for his guest and then opened a drawer in his desk. He pulled out a sheet of paper and tossed it to Davis. The rectangular sheet floated across the desk and landed face up.

"A wanted poster."

Abaddon sat down in his large padded leather chair. "Wes Clayton. Do you know him?"

"Heard of him."

"He is reputed to be the worst killer in Arizona. Which is to say the worst killer in the American Southwest. Which is to say, Wes Clayton is the worst killer on the continent – the best at what he does if you catch my meaning."

Davis grabbed the decanter and poured three fingers of Scotch whiskey. Abaddon smiled slightly at the rudeness. Davis killed his drink. "You want me to *collect* a man."

"Precisely, my boy, precisely. I want you to bring me the best criminal in the Americas."

"Wes Clayton? In one of your sheds?

Abaddon shook his head.

Davis said, "You'll send him out to do killin' for you?"

Abaddon's features hardened. He reached in the desk and pulled out another poster. He held it up and read out loud. "Wanted Dead or Alive. Lewton Davis. For the murder of five year old Tessie Stroud. Former Member of the Clayton Gang. Contact Nearest U.S. Marshal's Office."

Davis killed his drink. "It wasn't supposed to happen."

"It never is, Davis, it never is."

"That was a long time ago."

"The law does not forget."

"Is that what this here's about? You going to turn me in?"

"No, my boy, no. I just want you to realize that I have many resources at my disposal. Regardless of your position in relationship to the law, and to the, shall we say, rough and tumble environment in which you exist... I won't call it living... you have managed to keep your head when so many like you have not. You, sir, are resourceful and I need a resourceful man. You will of course receive proper remuneration for your labors."

"Remun...."

"Payment. You will be rewarded for your work. Handsomely."

"Wes Clayton. Dead or alive?"

"Dead. You will kill Wes Clayton. How is irrelevant to me, but kill him you must. You will preserve his head and hands. And any personal ornaments. Rings, watches – that sort of thing."

Davis looked over to the glass jar on the block of wood. "You're going to put him on display."

"Precisely."

Davis laughed. "How much?"

"Twenty-five thousand dollars."

"Jesus."

"Half when you bring in Clayton. The other half will be waiting in a bank in Mexico. When this task is completed, I want you out of the country, Davis."

"Yeah, I get it."

"Clayton was last seen—"

"I know where to find him, Mr. Abaddon."

Abaddon, reached back into his desk and brought out an envelope. He handed it over. "Funds to get you outfitted properly."

Davis took the envelope. "I'm outfitted."

"Then you'd best be on your way." It was a dismissal.

Davis turned and walked to the door. He stopped briefly and looked to one of the empty blocks of wood – a stand that would soon hold a preserved head in a glass jar, the head of an old friend.

***

The mining town of Rayburn, Arizona Territory was far busier underground than above. The mines clawed like skeletal fingers into the rock. The miners brought out copper colored wealth that kept them in whiskey and whores and that made men in far off eastern provinces wealthy beyond dreams. The main street was little more than a rubble strewn pathway hacked out of volcanic rock. Most of the houses were made of flat rock stacked like pancakes to make for fairly stable walls. Other, less fortunate men, slept in canvas tents or even back in the mines. Davis rode in barely noticed. He tied his mule in front of Bianculli's Angel Saloon and stepped inside.

Bianculli's provided the town's only real luxury and it was paltry luxury at that. The ornamentation was garish – designed to attract and hold the attention of miners escaping the harsh boredom of half-life in semi-darkness. Once his eyes adjusted to the light he looked over the place. Except for the bartender, the saloon was empty. The bartender was easy to recognize. Wes Clayton has cut his long hair and was parting it on the opposite side of his head. He had trimmed his long beard down to a narrow moustache. He looked like a completely different man. Davis stepped up.

Before he could speak, the bartender extended his hand and said, "Larsen, Gil Larsen, stranger. Barkeep, bouncer, mediator of disputes, and half-owner of the best bar in Rayburn. The look in his eyes showed he knew the identity of his new patron. "And you'd be...."

"Barnes, J.R. Barnes. Call me J.R."

"What's your poison, J.R?"

"Anything that won't kill me right off."

"That rather limits your selection. Try this." He reached behind the bar and retrieved a bottle of brown liquid. "Rum. I got it off a drummer who tried to cheat me on a pair of boots." He poured two shot glasses full. "On the house."

"What happened to the drummer?"

"Whatever is left of him is scattered from here to hell and back. Critters, you see."

"You wearing them boots?"

"I surely am."

"Not much of a going concern you have here."

"Once the day shifts end, things pick up considerably. What brings you to these parts, J.R?"

Davis glanced around, paying particular attention to the door, and spoke in a quiet voice. "You do, Wes." He leaned closer. "How would you like half of $25,000?"

"Killin' somebody important?"

"Nossir. I got a nice little scheme worked out, but I need you to pull it off."

"Gold shipment? Bank?"

Two miners walked through the door and marched to the far end of the bar. Clayton served them and returned to his old friend and his friend's offer.

Davis said, "I don't want to talk about it here."

"Bianculli comes in in a couple of hours. I'll be free then."

"You know that draw about a mile east of here, the one with a prospect up on the hill?"

"Yeah, I know it."

"Meet me there sundown or later."

"Twenty-five thousand dollars."

"It's over California way. Just waiting for us to take it."

Clayton rapped a shot glass on the bar. "Then let's go take it."

***

Davis brewed coffee over a small, smokeless fire as he watched the sundown. He sat down on a wooden cask he had left at the mining prospect before riding into Rayburn. A light rain to the south brought the smell of desert sage on the wind to mingle with the aroma of coffee. He made a cigarette and waited. As the long shadows merged with the coming night he heard the sound of a rider approaching.

"Davis! That you?"

"C'mon in."

Clayton rode into the campsite and dismounted. He tied his horse next to Davis' mount and walked to the fire. "Coffee ready?"

"Help yourself."

"Believe I will." He grabbed one of two cups off a flat rock placed next to the campfire. "You?"

"In a minute."

"Why are you bringing me in on this deal, Lewt?"

"You saved my life that time down in Bisbee."

Clayton shrugged.

"Well, I figure I owe you. Besides you're the only other man who can make sure my plan works."

"I'm listening."

"This side of San Diego, about thirty miles give or take, this here man, he's got this hacienda full of... well all kinds of rich stuff. And money, Wes, more money enough to burn a wet mule. And then some."

"And how do we go about getting all this money?"

"We just walk in and take it. I know he's got twenty-five thousand. He's got to have more. I can get us inside where I know he's got the cash hid."

"What's so special about me that you're offering me this... gift?"

"I can't do it without you, Wes."

Davis lowered his head as if staring at the ground. His eyes looked toward his friend. Clayton wrapped both hands around his coffee cup. Davis pulled his Colt and fired. The shot hit Clayton dead center of his chest, knocking him back into the fire. Davis pulled the hammer on his revolver back and fired again. Another shot hit dead center. He moved quickly to drag Clayton off the fire. As he pulled the man away he noticed his friend's blood mixing with the spilled coffee.

He wasted no time in spreading the dead man on the rock. He put on his work gloves. Using a large knife retrieved from his horse he used a rock as a hammer and quickly chopped off Clayton's hands. The head had to be sliced below the Adam's apple until the blade met bone. Again, the rock served as a hammer to finish the job.

Davis used the knife to pry open the cask he had been sitting on. It was filled nearly to the rim with alcohol. He dropped Clayton's hands into the cask and then lowered the head in, neck first. He hammered the lid on tight and then walked over to the smoldering fire where he pulled a small lidded pot from the coals. He pried off the lid and poured the contents, tar, around the lid of the cask to seal it.

A shot in the desert night isn't an unusual event and the likelihood of someone coming to investigate the noise was negligible. Davis didn't take that chance. Moments later he road down the wash, leading his friend's horse, which carried the cask. An hour later he was out of the mountains and into the flat desert leading to Mesa City. Outside the city he transferred the cask to his own horse. He rode into the city, sold Wes's horse and moved on without stopping for the food he needed or the whiskey he craved.

California and $25,000 were just a few days away.

***

Davis woke up to the sound of his horse's hooves clicking on the slick rock of a dry creek bed just below his camp. He sat up and grabbed his pistol. He slid on his boots and ran down toward the wash. A few hundred yards away an Indian boy led the animal toward the desert. He carried the cask under his arm. When he came out of the wash and into the open an old woman and a young girl rushed to him. The woman took the reins of the horse. The young girl ran to the boy. Each took up an end of the cask and followed the woman and the horse into the desert.

The trio of Indians moved slowly. Davis caught up with them in less than a minute. When the Indians heard his approach, the woman handed the reins to the children. They moved away quickly while the woman pulled a knife and ran toward Davis. She howled like a maddened banshee. She was scrawny from malnourishment. Her hair was as wild as her eyes. One bullet between those eyes ended the charge. Ahead, the boy dropped the cask into the sand. It barely missed landing on a sharp rock. Davis' second shot of the day took off the side of the young boy's head. He twisted in a half circle as he fell.

The girl, the youngest and scrawniest of the lot, tried to climb on to the saddle. She could not have been older than ten. One shot in the middle of her back ended the effort. She shrieked as she fell back and spooked the horse. The animal reared slightly and loped into the desert. Davis ran to the body of the old woman – dead. The boy and the girl showed no signs of life when he kicked them. He squatted down on one knee and examined the cask. He smiled.

"It looks like you'll make it, Wes."

He looked to the desert and felt a cold chill hit his stomach. His horse was down, shrieking in pain. Davis double-checked the cask for leaks or breakage. Satisfied, he rushed into the desert to his horse. The animal had stumbled into a prairie dog hole. Its right leg was broken. Davis' fourth kill shot of the day put an end to its suffering.

He returned to the cask, created a makeshift back pack and hoisted his former friend's remains on his back.

"Thirty miles or so, Wes. I reckon I can do that afoot."

Davis walked all day, guided by an excellent sense of direction, his knowledge of the land made while riding east to Arizona and Wes Clayton. The hacienda would be easy to find. His pace was confident.

The confidence wore off as the day wore on. A hot sun sapped what little energy was left over from scrambling up the rugged path through the mountains. When his horse fell, it landed on and crushed his canteen. Thirst and the danger of dehydration were serious threats. He followed an old and little used road that would eventually lead to a broad plain and Abaddon's hacienda. He drank stagnant water from fetid pools when he was lucky enough to find them. The water made him sick, but he marched on.

"Up the hill... over the hill... down the hill... get my money...." The cadence kept him moving and kept his mind off the thirst and pains of desert hiking. He continued walking well past dark until his stumbling and falling presented a real danger of cracking the cargo strapped to his back.

"All right. All right, Wes." At times he felt as if his head was a paper bag full of bees. At other times his mind almost refused to work. Simple decisions became confusing obstacles to progress. More than once he spent unnecessary time deciding which way to take around a boulder fallen in the trail. His voice was as cracked and raspy as his parched throat. "Get you... new home... tomorrow, Wes." His laugh turned into a painful, wracking cough. "Get me...." He stopped, nearly falling from his own sudden lack of momentum. He tried to swallow without success. "... everything."

Sleep, forced by exhaustion, came easy. Waking up, forced by pain, was just as easy. He struggled up, strapped the cask to his back and moved into the rocky path. By the end of the day he was stumbling downhill. Sundown caught him leaning against a large boulder.

"Damn, you, Wes! Get off my back."

He forced a dry laugh.

"Get it, Wes... off my back?"

He fell down, lacking the strength to remove the weight. He closed his eyes. The world was dark when he opened them. At first he thought he was seeing spots before his eyes. He leaned forward on all fours and shook his head.

"Lights, Wes."

Below the world was dark except for a square of glowing yellow lights – lanterns.

"The hacienda. We made it."

Davis forced himself to wait until false dawn. That dim twilight made walking far safer than stumbling, and possibly dying, in the dark.

"Almost... there...."

He was within a mile of the hacienda when he heard the bell. He had fallen to his knees and was searching for some last resource of strength, some energy that would enable the final walk. Shouts followed the clanging of the bell. He blinked. The painful movement was like scratching his eyes with sand. Several men, Mexican peons, ran toward him. Each carried a canteen.

"We made it, Wes."

Davis fainted and fell into the dust.

***

"How are you, my boy?" Abaddon stepped into the small, but well apportioned room where Davis had spent the night.

"I've been better. But I've been worse, too." He sat on the edge of the bed and pulled on his boots.

"Your recuperative powers are truly amazing, my boy."

"That's what that doctor of yours said. 'Re-coop something."

"Dr. Prince is one of my staff. I got him after the war. I made certain arrangements so that he could avoid all that Andersonville trouble. He'll never leave my service."

"Yeah. About my money."

"Of course. Why do you not complete your dressing and join me and the good doctor in my sanctum sanctorum."

"You're what?"

"Jefferson, my houseboy will show you the way."

"Five minutes."

"Take your time, my boy. You have all the time in the world."

"My money?"

"Your reward for a job well done awaits, my boy." He snapped his fingers out in the hall way. A tall Negro man appeared as if from nowhere. Abaddon spoke to him in polite, but firm tones. "Jefferson, when Mr. Davis is ready, show him downstairs."

The Negro nodded.

A minute or so later he led Davis to the descent into Abaddon's so-called holy of holies. Abaddon and Prince stood near the Kodiak bear. Abaddon motioned Davis in, moving toward the large desk at the same time. He reached into the cabinet and brought out a bottle of liquor. He poured a double shot and handed it to Davis. "More of that single malt you seem to enjoy. This one is a little more potent. I hope it is to your liking."

Davis took it, sipped, and then finished it off. "About my money, Mr. Abaddon."

"Of course. Everything is ready for you. But, please, join me and Dr. Prince for a farewell drink – a bon voyage for your journey so to speak." He poured another couple of shots. Prince joined them at the desk.

Davis looked around the room. "Where's Wes? I figured you'd have him on display by now." He felt a brief half-moment of dizziness and braced himself against the edge of the desk.

Abaddon nodded to Prince who stepped over to the large cabinet and retrieved his doctor's bag.

Davis looked across the room. The glass jar for his friend's head was empty.

Abaddon spoke dismissively. "I had Jefferson toss it to the coyotes."

Davis turned, incredulous. "You paid me... you're paying me—"

"I am paying you nothing, Mr. Davis. I have bought you."

"I don't...." He waivered at the edge of the desk.

Abaddon said, "I collect only the best Mr. Davis. You have – magnificently – bested the best gunman in the Southwest."

Prince removed a slim, rectangular pouch from his bag. He opened it to reveal a surgical kit. "That makes you the best, doesn't it, Mr. Davis?"

Davis reeled, overtaken by dizziness. He swayed and struggled to hang on to the desk. He lost the battle, lost consciousness and fell to the floor.

Abaddon pulled a cord hanging near the cabinet and said, "Jefferson will assist you in carrying Mr. Davis to your operating room, doctor. Please leave as much of the neck and wrists as possible. Check his pockets for any trinkets of interest."

"Yes, sir, Mr. Abaddon."

Jefferson arrived and he and Prince carried Davis from the room. Abaddon sat down and pulled two brass plates from a drawer. "Wes Clayton." He sniffed and tossed it into a trash receptacle. He held the other to the light and smiled. Abaddon stood up, crossed the room and put the brass plate against the glass jar. "Only the best, Mr. Davis. I collect only the best."

PLEW'S DEAD

Link Baigent and Henry Smith rode into the canyon leading to Hewitt City. Smith said, "You're going to like Hewitt City. Lots of whiskey and nobody asks questions." As they entered the edge of the small mining community they noticed that something was wrong.

The rock-strewn path that passed for the road in front of Bark's Saloon was crowded. Store owners, workers and most if not all of the town's miners milled around, but apparently with some purpose. Their faces reflected anger and their hands held rifles, shotguns or pistols. A blank cartridge of a man who called himself the Pecos Kid leaned against a wall at the edge of the excitement. A big man stepped up on a block of wood that passed for a chair and shouted for attention. Level Compton's voice was lost in a continuing wave of anger and he failed miserably to stem the tide. He looked around for support and found it in the town's conscience. The old man called Eli stepped up on a block of wood and raised his arms. The rabble slowly became quiet and Eli's voice carried easily over the men. "Everyone that is of the truth heareth my voice." The men grew quiet. "Let us hear the truth and let us judge and act only according to the truth." He turned to a man standing next to Compton – a miner, but not from Hewitt City – Halsey he was called. He was one of many who worked their own dry diggings alone or with a single partner. A white bandage, soiled with his own blood, was wrapped around his head. Eli stepped down and offered the man his place on the block. "Speak, brother Halsey and mind you to the truth."

The man stepped up and spoke forcefully and with emotion. "Them bastards at Denada done killed old Plew. They damn near killed me."

"Plew's dead!"

"Yessir."

"When!"

Eli raised his arms to quiet the crowd. Halsey continued. "Not mor'n two hours ago. They just showed up and killed Plew. I was in the mine or they'd have got me, too."

One of the miners shook his head. "Plew...."

Halsey nodded. "Graveyard dead."

"Sons a bitches!"

"They've gone too far this time!"

"We gonna take this? Again!"

Eli raised his arms and again Halsey was allowed to speak. Little flecks of spittle formed at the corners of his mouth and his voice became more emotional with every word. "I took a chance and made a run for it. That's when I got this." He pointed to his head.

"Is it the whole Denada bunch? How many!"

"Don't know, but I 'spect it's all of 'em. Ten at least."

"Damn!"

"Old Plew...."

Halsey placed his hand on Eli's shoulder. He wavered slightly. "It's come down to them or us, boys."

Compton turned to face the men. "He's right. Them or us. Or we might as well pack it in and move on – tails between our legs."

Halsey stepped off the block, appearing woozy. Eli and Compton helped him down, but appeared lost as to what to do next. The rabble broke into small groups, but the need for violence and revenge ruled the moment. All faces turned to Smith as the two riders arrived. Link spoke softly. "Looks like Hewitt City is in need of a little tinkerin.'"

"I don't need this."

"Yeah, but you're the unofficial official. Look at those faces."

The blacksmith took their horses' reins. He looked to Smith. "You better get in there. Unless some bloke takes charge, we're going to have a riot on our hands." The blacksmith paused to kick the dirt. "I'll tend to your horses. You tend to this bunch." He walked away as Smith and Link approached the saloon.

Link spoke in a low voice. Who the hell is this Plew?"

Smith spoke quickly. Halsey and him have been partnered up nearly ten years. He's—"

"What are you going to do," shouted one of the miners.

"We can't do nothing for Plew."

This here crowd ain't going to just melt away," Smith. "I see that."

Compton said, "Let's get inside, Smith. We got to get a handle on this."

He led the way. The crowd followed and Link was quickly edged aside. In less than a minute there were only two outsiders to the event – Link and the Pecos Kid. Neither made an effort to join the other. The men hammered Smith with questions, but he was not given time for answers. He at last called for help. Eli stood back up on the block of wood. "Brothers, allow the man time to speak."

He stepped off and gestured for Smith to take his place.

Smith thought, *Run like hell or step up? Damn this town.* He stepped on a chair and the men grew quiet. He took his time in looking over the men before speaking, commanding actually. "Are you men ready to kill these sons a' bitches!"

"I've had it with these bastards!"

"Let's end it now!"

"Get it over and done with!

Smith raised his arms for quiet. "We ain't going to take this, boys. I promise. But give me a minute to think this through. We can't just mount up and ride in there without some of us getting killed unnecessary-like." He stepped down and walked to Bark's door. "Compton. Bark. Come in here with me. You, too, Halsey." The men followed. Link slipped in behind them.

They pulled a few barrels up next to the bar. Link rolled one over and joined them.

Smith raised his hand slightly. "This ain't none of your affair, Link. You can sit this one out."

"Not likely. You saved my hide the other day."

"We're clear, Link."

"Seems like that's my decision, ain't it?"

"You up for a ride and a fight?"

"I'll hold up my end."

Eli, who had been standing near the door, stepped in. "Brothers, you must not give in to random violence. 'And with what measure ye mete, it shall be measured to you again.'"

Smith shook his head. "Meat? What the hell does he mean, meat? We ain't none of them cannibals."

Bark frowned and then his face relaxed. "Judgment. He means we can't just take the law into our own hands."

Smith snorted. "The hell we can't."

Compton slapped his hand against the bar. "We'll give 'em judgment, Eli. The same judgment they gave old Plew and too many others."

Eli raised his hands. "I agree with your intent. It is your methods I cannot sanction."

Bark spoke. "We can't wait for the law, Eli. Even if we find the sheriff and even if he's sober and even if he'll bother himself to leave his whores, he won't get here for a day or more. The Denada gang will be back in their snake den by then."

Compton nodded. "We'll never blast 'em out of there. Not without getting a bunch of us killed."

Eli stepped forward half a pace. "Still, we must not act outside the law lest we be judged as outside the law."

Bark scratched his head. "Eli's got a point. The sheriff could come for us after we conclude our... business."

Smith stood up, crossed the room and poured a shot glass full of whiskey. He downed it in a single swallow. "Damn it. I've had it with the 'law.' If you want an end to this business, end it. End it now." He pulled out his pistol and checked his cartridges to emphasize the point.

Bark puffed his cheeks. "What'll we do?"

Link sat forward. "Miner's court."

Compton sat upright. "Of course!"

"I don't understand," said Bark.

Compton smiled as he explained. "When there's no official law in a mining camp, the miner's form a miner's court. It's legal."

"Legal enough," Smith said. He killed another shot and returned to the group. He brought the bottle and several shot glasses with him. A round was quickly poured and consumed.

Compton brought up the obvious. "We need a judge—"

"Eli." Link and Bark spoke at the same time.

Compton continued, "And a jury."

Link looked around the small group. "All present and accounted for."

Compton handed Eli a glass of whiskey. "Eli?"

Eli accepted the offering and drank quickly. He seemed to be in deep thought as he extended his arm. Compton poured another shot. This time Eli finished it in two sips. "What are the charges, gentlemen."

Compton spoke with genuine conviction. "Murder, your honor. Old Plew and others too numerous to mention."

"Are there any witnesses? Brother Halsey?"

Halsey wiped a spot of dried blood from the corner of his eye. "They killed Plew and damn near killed me, Eli... your honor."

Eli turned to the other men. "The witness has spoken. What say ye, the jury?"

Compton spoke first. "Guilty as charged." Smith, Bark, and Link said the same.

Halsey spoke last. "Guilty sons of bitches."

Eli shook his head. "You cannot cast your lot, Brother Halsey. You are a principle witness."

"Yessir. Still...."

"Enough. The court is ready to pronounce its sentence." He extended his arm again. Compton poured some more of the judge's fee. Eli sipped slowly. "Guilty as charged." He stood up. "You men continue your work. I will inform the assembly." He stepped outside and moved into the crowd.

Smith leaned forward, an action duplicated by the other men. "Halsey, you think they're still at that half-ass tunnel of yours you call a mine?"

"Yeah. They was already hittin' their tangle leg when I skeedaddled. They'll be drunkern' a pack of reservation Injuns tonight and hung over tomorrow."

"In the mine?"

"I built a shack. Most likely they'll be in there." He sniffed, wiped his nose and squinted as if looking carefully at something in the distance. "One door. No windows. Just a chimney."

"We'll hit 'em when the sunrise is on 'em. Bark, you and Compton find a couple of spots on the trail leading in. One on each side."

The two men nodded. Bark spoke. "I'm in for sure, Smith, but I ain't much of a shot."

Smith nodded. "Carry your side arms, both of you, but use your shotguns for the work we got to do."

"Agreed," said Compton.

Smith looked to Halsey again. "Your digs pretty much the same since I was by there?"

"Yessir. I cleaned up a bit. It's pretty damn open for say ten yards around the mine 'n the shack."

Link spoke up. "My old man used to call that a field of fire."

Smith snorted. "That's what we'll make it, then. Link, you and me will edge our way up and over the mine.

Compton and Bark will get 'em coming and we'll get 'em going."

Compton pounded his right fist into his left palm. "That'll do."

Halsey spoke up. "What about me?"

Smith shook his head.

Halsey measured out his words slowly. "After what they did to Plew, there ain't no ways in hell you're keepin' me out of this fight. If I have to I'll ride out now."

"All right, Halsey. But you stay with the horses. Keep 'em quiet. Agreed?"

"I do not agree."

"Get a rope, Compton. We'll tie him up and let some of the boys keep an eye on him until we get back."

"All right, damn it. I'll watch the damn horses. You just make sure you men kill 'em. Kill every last one of 'em."

"This time tomorrow there won't be no Denada gang."

Smith stood up. "We need to head out now and get our sleep in the mountains."

Bark stood up. The others followed his lead. "Why don't we just rest up here, Smith? It's a hell of a lot more comfortable than—"

"Those men out there need to see us movin' on. Hell, otherwise half of 'em will do something crazy on their own. They'll be the sumbitches caught in that field of fire."

"You're right. Damn you," Bark said.

Halsey said, "I'll get the horses."

Link said, "Get mules. They're better for this kind of work."

"I'll get the mules, then." He walked toward the door. His steps were shaky.

Smith said, "You men know what you need. Get it and we'll meet back here. Make it quick before those hotheads out there get frisky."

Halsey was halfway across the room when Link called out. "Halsey. You say you got a chimney in that shack."

"Yessir. It's just stacked up flat rocks, but it does the job."

Link grinned and slapped Smith on the back. "We just got an edge. Come on. I'll explain while we pack. But first I got to make a run up to Tosie's.

***

Link left Tosie's Restaurant with a couple of sacks in hand. He tied them to his saddle, mounted up and met Smith and the others near the edge of town. The miners were more subdued now that the "law" was taking action. Their anger smoldered and several offered to join the party. Eli's presence and his common sense reined in those few determined at all costs to revenge the murder of Plew. The old man raised his arms to the posse. "Not the hearers of the law are just before God, but the doers of the law shall be justified in his sight."

Bark and Compton spoke at the same time. "Amen."

"Let's go," Smith said.

Link pulled on his horse's reins and led the party south and out of town. They followed the road for about a mile and began riding into the shadows cast by a setting sun. Full darkness arrived before Link led them to a fairly wide and flat area under a large cottonwood. "Let's fix some grub and grab a few hours of sleep. I want to be ready before sun up."

Bark, Compton and Halsey dismounted quickly. Smith edged closer to Link. Each remained in the saddle. Smith spoke in a quiet, determined voice. "Who made you boss regulator?"

"Take over."

Smith grinned. "Hell, no. I like somebody else making the decisions."

"Not exactly like old times, eh?"

"Tired of getting friends killed."

"I know the feeling. Let's settle in."

"Whatever you say. Boss."

Halsey tended to the horses. Compton and Bark settled in and were eating on some biscuits Bark brought along. Link and Smith shared some beef jerky. Night had fallen, but all agreed on the foolishness of building a fire.

Compton looked at Link's saddlebags. "What's in the sacks, Link?"

"An edge."

"What kind of edge?"

"One that might work."

"I mean—"

Smith tossed a small twig at Compton's boot. "The kind he'll tell us about when he's ready.

Link looked up to the stars. "Ya'll get some sleep. I'll take first watch. Smith?"

"Yeah. I got the second."

"That'll do. We'll get moving about an hour before false dawn."

Bark, Compton and Halsey bedded down. Smith made a smoke, carefully hiding the lighting of it behind a large rock, the flame cupped in his hands. He smoked quickly beneath a scrubby mesquite, the limbs and leaves dissipating the smoke and the smell of tobacco. When he finished, he eased over to Link's position back in the darkness next to the rock wall near the campsite. Link was whittling a pile of wood shavings on his blanket. Smith spoke in a low voice. "Leaving before false dawn will put is at Halsey's mine a good bit before sunrise."

"That'll give me just enough time."

"What you got in mind, Link?

"I figure that Denada bunch will be drunk or hungover."

"Count on it."

"But they still outnumber us. I don't like the odds."

"What's this edge of yours?"

"You'll see."

"Damn you."

"Before you sack out bring me a couple of river rocks."

"Rocks?"

"One flat and smooth. One of 'em round and smooth."

"Sure thing. May I kiss your ass while we're at it?"

"Git."

Moments later Smith was snoring lightly. Unlike the three "townies crowded in the center of the camp, he slept several yards back from the others.

Link put his wood shavings into a flour sack. He removed a handful of red chili pods from another sack and started grinding them into powder on the smooth rocks Smith brought. Several handfuls later he dumped the chili power in with the wood shavings. He took a can of oil from his saddlebag and poured it in with the dry ingredients. He mixed it up well and then tied off the bundle with a rawhide strip before dry-washing his hands in the sand. Link held up the sack and smiled. "This is going to hurt."

He slept well after Smith relieved him on watch and was well-rested when awakened at the appointed hour. The two men woke the others. They saddled up and rode out without saying a word. Halsey's camp was less than a mile away on the other side of a ridge. They made good time, halting at a place on the other side of a ridge that overlooked the mine. Link dismounted and the others followed his lead.

He looked to Halsey. "Is there a trail or an animal run up over the backside of your mine?"

"Yeah. I'll lead yo—"

"You'll stay with the horses."

"Damn it, those bastards shot Plew."

Smith put his hands on Halsey's shoulder. "And we're gonna shoot those bastards."

"You can't make me sta—"

"No," Link said.

Smith tapped Halsey again. "He's right. You're in bad shape. If you stumble, knock loose a rock or something you could give us away."

Compton handed his reins to Halsey. "We get the sons of bitches."

Halsey let out a breath of air and took all the reins. "I'll tie 'em off over there. You boys be careful." He pointed to a large boulder with a huge crack down the middle. "There's a deer run behind that rock. It leads up the hill and over the mine. You can follow it easy in the dark."

"All right. Compton, you and Bark work your way down the road and up to the mine. Find a couple of places where you can get 'em in a cross fire."

Bark said, "When do you want us to start shooting?"

"When they come at you."

"Oh, Lord," Bark said.

"You'll do all right," Smith said.

Link pointed to the road. "Get going. Walk slow and be quiet. No talking when you get there."

"Then they'll come after us," Compton said.

"Toward you, not at you. They'll come toward you 'cause they'll be running scared," Link said.

Bark cleared his throat. "Then what?"

Smith spit before speaking. "Let nature take its course."

"Ya'll get going," Link said. The two men, shotguns in hand, took to the road as Halsey hobbled the horses.

Link, his sack in hand, turned and headed toward the split rock and the deer run behind it. Smith followed. The trail was easy to follow, but the going was slow over the rocky hill. Neither man wanted to start a rock rolling down the hill – an alarm that might even wake up a few drunks. The dim, gray light of false dawn was upon the hills when they reached the trail just over Halsey's mine. They took up a commanding position at the highest point.

Seven horses were hobbled near the shack, but no men were in sight. The two men waited, but the only man they saw was a drunk who stumbled out of the shack to urinate on an ocotillo. "That'll stunt your growth," he mumbled. The man turned and tripped and nearly fell to the ground. He stopped and oriented himself and then stumbled back into the shack.

Above, Smith whispered. "If they're all as bustheaded as that SOB, our work is half done."

"You gonna give 'em a chance?"

"Yeah. The same chance they gave this old Plew."

"When do you want to hit 'em?"

"Right when the sun hits 'em."

"That's what I figured, too."

Link looked over the ledge. No one moved below and the only sound was the mumbling of a few drunks in the shack. "You know we're gonna have to do most of the work. Probably all of it."

Smith looked over the ledge. Bark and Compton had taken positions on each side of the road and well hidden by piles of tailings. "They're good men. They know what to do."

Later, as the dim gray in the eastern sky turned light pink and then gold, movement stirred in the shack below. Smoke and the smell of burning bacon rose from the chimney and the mumbling voices became louder. Link grabbed the sack he had prepared. "Hand me some Lucifers."

Smith gave him a half dozen matches. "I think I done figured out what you're gonna do with that sack. If they don't hear you and run outside to blow your damn head off."

"We don't need that bunch making a stand in that mine. This here'll get 'em out in the open."

Link stood up, but in bent into a low crouching position and started down the slope toward the shack. He moved slowly, traversing the hill one careful step at a time. He couldn't keep all the rocks from sliding, but most stopped before dropping off. The few that did fall landed quietly in the dirt. The old shack had been built so close to the edge of the mine that someone could step from the hill to the roof. Link picked up a broken tree branch about the length and wide of his arm and stepped over. His movements were slow as if he was sneaking up on a coiled rattler. Fortunately, the roof was nearly flat. He was next to the chimney in three steps.

He looked down toward Bark and Compton. He caught Bark's eye and nodded. Bark waved across the road. Compton stuck his head up, waved quickly and ducked back. A quick glance above and back showed that Smith already had his Winchester aimed at the open area in front of the shack. Link untied his sack and dumped the contents down the smoking chimney, turning his head to keep the dark red dust from flying into his eyes. He placed the sack on top as a seal and put the tree limb down to hold it in place. He moved to the edge of the roof, took his pistol in hand and waited.

Inside, voices were at first confused, then angry and then panicked. The ground chili pods smoldered and put out a massive amount of painful, stinging smoke. The door opened and two men stumbled out. Link cocked his .45, but didn't fire. *Wait for it.* Two more men stumbled out before someone inside shouted. "Wait, you sumbitches!" Another voice replied, "I'm burning. Get out!" Another man rushed out, but he was going for his pistol.

Smith fired and the man fell with a bullet in his chest. Another man rushed out, a rifle in his hands. He fired, but was too blinded to see any targets. One of his companions was hit in the thigh. He, too fell. The last man rushed out. He held two pistols, but was rubbing his eyes on his shirt sleeves. Link fired and hit the man three times – once in the gut, once in the chest and once in the shoulder. As the other armed man turned to the sound of Link's gunfire, Smith shot again. The back of the target's head exploded. The remaining men dashed forward, but ran into Bark and Compton. Both men fired. The men in front of the shack were running or crawling, unable to fight back, unable to see, and unable to escape. Bark and Compton fired again as if killing a couple of dogs in the street. In less than half a minute all seven were spread out on the ground. All were dead. The Denada gang was dead.

Smith came down the hill quickly and joined Link who had jumped to the ground. He examined each of the Denada men to make sure they were all dead.

Bark and Compton joined up. Bark kicked one of the dead men's feet. "I've seen worse. Little Round Top."

"Fredericksburg," said Compton.

The two older men took the gun belts and pistols from the Denada bunch and pulled the bodies over to the edge of the cleared area. "What'll we do with 'em," Bark said. Compton shook his head. "That's Halsey's problem. We've done our work." They moved across the clearing and stood with Link and Smith. Halsey arrived with the horses moments later. The four men approached and were about to mount up when Halsey spoke. "You leaving now?"

Link was the first to respond. "I'm about all out of good deeds for the day, Halsey."

"Besides, Bark's buying when we get back to the saloon."

Bark nodded. "It's a fair day for getting drunk."

"What about Plew," Halsey said.

Compton said, "Damnation. We forgot about ol' Plew."

"Where is he," Smith said.

Halsey pointed to the far edge of the clearing, to a tailing pile. "They dumped him over

there. You boys got to help me give him a right proper burying. You can do that, can't you?"

"I ain't one for funerals," Link said.

Smith shook his head. "Me neither."

Bark spoke up. "Me 'n Compton, here, we'll help you see to the burying. These boys have done enough."

Compton stepped over to Link and Smith. He shook each man's hand. "Ol' Plew meant a lot to Halsey, here. Hell, everybody liked him. Those Denada boys earned what happened to them – for this and for a lot of other things."

"Ride out and start the services at the saloon on my account. We'll be by directly to

catch up," Bark said. He turned to Compton. "Let's go." The two men walked to the tailings pile. Halsey stared, immobile. He was weeping.

Link and Smith mounted their horses and eased on toward the road. They stopped and turned just as Bark and Compton were dragging Plew's body into the clearing. Compton grabbed a blanket from his horse and covered the body of the large German Shepherd.

"A dog!" Link's eyes widened. "We fought a war over a dog!"

Smith looked at the scene with no emotion on his face. "We've both seen wars fought for less."

They both watched the sad proceedings for a moment. Smith finally spoke. "At least with this war we get free drinks for a day."

"But... a dog?"

"Didn't you ever have a pet, Link?"

"A dog. A damn dog."

"I liked that dog."

The young men had enough respect for the dead to hold their laughter until they were on the other side of the hill and out of earshot.

PISSED

Celia Greene was healthy and small enough to be considered a "sweet young thang" by Western standards. Teenage boys and a few dirty old men, were already noticing the early signs of the woman soon to flower within her small frame. She was just old enough to go into town with her older brothers and just young enough to be considered a real pain, someone to be sent home by herself as soon as possible. The brothers gave her a penny to buy a few sticks of hard candy and then ran off the moment she'd entered the store. The little girl shrugged it off. Her mamma would get the full story with a bit of elaboration and a few tears tossed in for effect. Her brothers would pay dearly for such neglect. She started walking home, a small house located on the outskirts of Privy, A.T.

The Killer watched from the shade of a cottonwood at the edge of a wash. His mule was hobbled and out of sight. The Killer was the most wanted man in the territory. And the most dangerous because his face was unknown and he killed for no discernable reason. None of the wanted posters scattered throughout the territory bore an image or a description. He was a ghost with a knife.

The Killer's motivation was as simple as his method. He killed because someone pissed him off.

"The barkeep pissed me off."

"The whore pissed me off."

"The padre pissed me off."

Celia Greene has just pissed him off.

Jarvis Morrow watched the girl dancing down the road, but he didn't see The Killer. Morrow was the grounds keeper of the small, adobe church built nearer to God on a rise too small to be called a hill. A stand of mesquite trees and a thick wall of brownish-green shrubbery protected the old building from the waves of dust blowing in from the desert. The building and the grounds were in need of tending. No one was around. Morrow spit on the floor of the church and went back to the business at hand. Pilfering the previous Sunday's meager collection.

The Killer He made tracks for the girl and caught up with her at the edge of town. She was friendly and open and willing to walk a ways with a stranger. He smelled funny, but he seemed nice.

Celia was curious. "What 'cha doing, mister?"

He replied with a lie and a promise. Neither was important except that the child believed him, and within minutes she was happily on her way into the stand of trees behind the church in the company of a crooked little man with a crooked little face and the cold, hungry eyes vulture.

Inside the old church the same look graced the drawn features of Jarvis Morrow. He had just completed a round of his occasional letter writing to his ex-wives. Morrow was a retired tent preacher who had seen much of the Southwest in his sixty-nine years. In his time he had managed to see many of the region's most faithful and attractive ladies, too, and in the twilight of his life he remained overly-married, out of jail, just ahead of the law, and totally unrepentant.

He spoke to himself as he robbed his church. "'Withhold not good from them to whom it is due,' says the Good Book, and I'm due, Reverend." He paused his pilfering and stared at the name of the current preacher scrawled on a letter. "Prick!" He took one more coin and spit again. He walked into the main part of the church where a painting of Christ seemed to look into his soul.

"I need the damn money."

The old man looked away and then back. "You done nothing for me. Nothing!"

He walked away, but before leaving he turned back. "I don't believe in you. Hear me! I don't...."

Morrow was nearly six feet tall and well-built. He would have been handsome throughout his sunset years except for the dark emptiness in his eyes. Somewhere along the straight and narrow he had lost a fortune, at least three wives and several children. All he had left was a lousy job and the tattered cloth that held together the pitiful remnant of his faith. He had been hired a year earlier as caretaker of the small church. No one else had applied for the job and he was almost a shoe-in except for the powerful force that was widow Darlene Agee. When she had first met Morrow she'd slowly approached him, raised her palm to block off the lower portion of his face, and stared into the window of his soul.

The man's eyes were dark and empty.

She'd dropped her hand and yelled, "Get him out of my church!" Her protests, which continued through the year, fell on deaf ears and the care of her Lord's house fell into the hands of a burnt-out, empty shuck of a near-dead soul. None of that mattered. He worked cheap.

Money was not Mrs. Agee's concern. "I tell you, that horrid little man will bring trouble into our house," she said to anyone willing to put up with the diatribe that inevitably followed.

Morrow dropped the coins in the collection plate of his vest and closed and locked the preacher's desk. "Hell, I earned it."

Morrow never visited his wives, never wrote them. When their frequent letters arrived he told the postmen they were notes from his cousins. Often the envelopes carried a few dollars wrapped inside a delicate note written in a gentle hand. It was the only contact they shared. All his children were grown. Each had tracked him down. Each had been utterly disappointed and each had eventually driven his memory to the far and most desolate regions of their minds. He didn't much care, really. They never sent him any money like the wives did.

"Ungrateful little bastards." Morrow stomped through the dark church into the yellow kitchen at the rear of the building. He made a pot of coffee and cursed his job. Several deacons had called about the poor condition of the church grounds. Summer monsoon rains had created a field of ruts in the hard packed desert sand. He could put off the Lord's yard work no longer. He took a long time to finish the coffee opened the back door. "What the hell?"

A white man was walking into the trees with a black girl and that could mean only one damnable thing. He recognized Celia Greene, the cute little squirt he called "the black Greene girl." He did not recognize the man. Morrow's gut clenched and he spit on the wooden steps. Few things could raise a fire in his saggy old belly, but "race-mixing" was at the top of the short-list. He didn't give a damn what a man did with his flock or family, but he drew the line of race deep in the sand. Few in Privy disagreed and those few who did kept their comments to themselves. Morrow could punch and he fought dirty.

He stormed out the door and past the small storage shed. "You two! What the hell's going on out there!"

The Killer stood his ground, but Celia Greene backed away, scared half out of her wits. Most of the kids living around the church called Morrow "the monster man." She danced away from The Killer and rushed into the safety of the old road. She turned and laughed before skipping away. Her house, her mamma, and a whipping for her brothers were just around the next curve. She danced all the way home, quickly and without looking back. She had escaped the monster man.

Morrow pissed off The Killer.

Morrow scowled. Up close, the man looked stronger, a more wiry subject, than he had originally thought. That's when he had his idea. "Why don't you help me level out these ruts in the church yard? I can pay a little." He dropped his voice into a more serious tone. "No need for me to call the sheriff about the trespass or the young black girl." He sounded almost kind.

The Killer recognized the not-so-subtle threat. That really pissed him off.

Morrow offered another carrot with the stick, promising pie and coffee when the job was done.

The Killer took a long time to answer, looking over his prospective employer from top to bottom.

Morrow led the man to the adobe tool shed, opened the door and stepped inside. The rough walls were decorated with old sling blades, scythes, hedge clippers, shovels, rakes and other tools, all rusting from infrequent use and poor care. "Seek and ye shall find, eh, Brother?" He was feeling around for the rusty old shovel when The Killer stepped into the darkness.

***

Widow Darlene Agee found Morrow's body the next day. Once a month it was her unpleasant duty to righteously confront Morrow and chastise him over his continual neglect of church property. She arrived mid-afternoon as usual. It was a time selected to gall the caretaker, who was given to frequent naps. She found him in the sanctuary. After the screaming, and after some of the deacons arrived, the deputy sheriff showed up. He was pointed to front door, but no one volunteered to walk inside with him. They assured him absolutely nothing had been touched.

The deputy was known as a real hard charger among the members of the force, yet he entered the dark sanctuary slowly, fearfully. The quiet, nervous behavior of the flock at the front door had spooked him. He stared. "Sweet Jesus!"

Jarvis Morrow lay stretched out on a bloody floor with his feet pointed to the door and

his head toward the pulpit. His right arm was stretched out and his hand open, as if reaching for something in the darkness. The deputy allowed his eyes to follow a straight line from the hand. It pointed directly to a crude painting of Jesus Christ. The deputy gagged as he bent down. Morrow's heart had been carved from his body.

The deputy, no longer a young man, made out his report properly and filed it according to proper procedure. The report eventually made the rounds to the sheriff's offices around the territory. By that time, however, it was merely another set of papers to be filed and, much like Jarvis Morrow, forgotten.

The Killer rode out of town unnoticed and by sundown was nearing the outskirts of Mesa City. A light shown through the window of a small adobe house. A man stepped out onto the rough plank porch, looked around, unbuttoned his britches and peed onto a nearby cactus. He looked up and saw the scrawny man on a scrawny mule and he waved.

The Killer stared back. The man really pissed him off.

PRINCESS DODU AND THE SHORTROUND

Hephaestus approached his mistress with all the show he could muster. He was a tall and stately Negro of indeterminate age and dressed as someone befitting the servant of Princess Dodu of Lorraine, a member of the minor European royalty. Her real name was Belle DelCour and Belle Decker and Belle Delotte and Belle LeCour and a few other names left in the dust of Arizona and New Mexico. She was a large and handsome woman dressed in what the citizens of McCloyville, Arizona Territory would take as the clothing European royalty. She was also a conniving whore practiced in deception, poison and the swift removal of money, gold or jewelry from any man with whom she had contact.

Her costume, regal bearing and the worshipful attention given by her manservant raised eyebrows and caused considerable gossip in the Balmore Hotel where she had taken up temporary residence.

Hephaestus presented her with a glass of brandy on a linen napkin in his palm. She accepted it with a nod of her head. He bent low to converse in privacy. "Our little friends are in dire straits, Princess. One, they are being tortured."

"Tortured?" It was a gasp.

"The guards here have a game in which they toss vipers and scorpions into the cells. The unfortunate inmates dare not make a move for hours at a time. It has proven a deadly 'game' on several occasions."

"Interesting. We should remember that technique."

Hephaestus stood erect as if allowing her time to think. The few other patrons in the hotel's reception area continually glanced toward the princess. When in public, Belle performed. She had to meet expectations if she was to execute her plans successfully. Bills had to be paid and a select group of wealthy men needed to be skinned. And quickly. She motioned her manservant closer. "I want them out of there."

"You're loyalty is admirable, Ma'am, but there are complications."

"What the hell would they be?"

"This mayor you've been keeping time with is most proud of his town. He is particularly proud of his jail."

She took a polite sip of her brandy. "That ain't all he's proud of." Her face registered scorn.

Hephaestus continued in an overly deferential manner, as if passing along the latest missive from the Province of Lorraine. "His jail is far stronger than most prisons in these parts."

"He's a big one for show, he is. Fetch me another drink."

"Yes, Ma'am." He marched off with all the dignity of his "office."

Belle organized her thoughts. Her tiny diminutive associates in crime, Short and Round, were caught red handed picking the pocket of Reverend Ford Belene, a man who preached, but did not much practice the art of forgiveness. He insisted on prosecution to the fullest extent of the law. After all, he said, the pair of ruffians had attempted to abscond with the funds from the most recent passing of the collection plate. No one thought to wonder why those funds were on the good reverend's person rather than in one of McCloyville's many banks. For whatever reasons, the pair known together as ShortRound had again received the short end of the stick.

Loyalty? She hadn't even thought about that. Did they feel loyalty to her or were they just riding the most convenient meal ticket? It didn't really matter. They knew her real identity and a good bit of her plans. She would not abandon them to a legal inquiry.

Hephaestus arrived with the second drink. He carried a newspaper under his arm. Again he bowed low in handing over the drink. Again he spoke in a low voice. "Ma'am, we should be leaving California as soon as practicable."

"We leave as soon as I figure out how to get ShortRound back. I'll work through Mayor Redlich. He's a gullible old fool."

"We haven't time, Ma'am."

She accepted the glass and the napkin with grace. "What's up?"

"A patron just arriving from the west spoke with the hotel manager. It seems that Sheriff Arlen and his deputies were taken violently ill after our departure from their township. Arlen and that deputy, Wes, are dead. The other one, Conly, survived and is acting sheriff. Belle Delotte and her 'educated negro servant' are wanted for questioning, as are two midgets who are suspected of being traveling companions of said Delotte and said negro. The newspapers from the west arrive day after tomorrow, Princess."

She finished the brandy and stood up. "Come." She marched outside.

Hephaestus bowed and followed.

McCloyville was busting at the seams. Silver had been discovered in the nearby hills just six months earlier. A withered stage stop had boomed to a town of more than 1500 miners, whores, pimps, thieves, killers, drummers and shopkeepers. Fortunately, too many people were busy trying to make too much money to pay much attention to Princess Dodu and her entourage. The arrival of newspapers would quickly change all that. She stopped and looked around the town as if considering purchasing some or all of it. The performance continued even under stress. She looked at Hephaestus and said quietly, "Have you had a look at the jail?"

"I have, Ma'am, and it is a veritable fortress: an adobe wall two feet thick and seven feet high surrounds the jail building. That wall is topped with strands of that new barbed wire, which adds another two feet to its height."

"And the jail itself?"

"An adobe structure. Two cells. No windows. Iron-reinforced doors. Sadistic guards who are well armed. I do not see how anyone can escape such a structure."

A horse tied to a nearby rail offered a comment on the situation. The opinion splattered in the sand with a modest thump. A number of fat flies made it their new residence. Belle looked at Hephaestus. "Go back for a second look at that jail."

"And what shall I be looking for, Ma'am?"

She whispered the answer. He nodded and moved away. Belle ambled back into the hotel. Princess Dodu needed another drink.

***

They discussed the situation when Hephaestus brought her meal to her room. She was living on credit that she'd purchased with a few favors promised to the hotel's owner The Princess was taking full advantage of the man's gullibility. More than ever she enjoyed making fools out of men. It was so easy.

"You think they can squeeze through?" She spoke softly. The walls were thin and one never knew who was on the other side.

"Their diminutive size makes that route of escape a certainty save for two concerns."

"Those are?"

"One, the exit point is barred by iron. They could conceivably loosen the metal. It's just an adobe wall, but they would need a sharp implement. Two, there are two guards during the day. One at night. Mr. Short and Mr. Round are vicious little weasels, but I do not see how they can overpower a large, well-armed ruffian. Again, some sort of weapon would be required."

Belle cut into her steak. The food was surprisingly good for a town so far from the coast and civilization. As she chewed the rare beef she poked the round end of a baked potato with her knife and stirred it in the blood on her plate. A smile formed and her eyes brightened. "You've done some acting, ain't you?"

"Performing talent was one of my many skills back on the plantation. You've seen my work."

She slid the round end of potato over the point of the knife. "You ever had a woman dogways?" Her eyes locked on to his.

"If you mean—" He stopped in mid-sentence as their eyes met. She wasn't talking about sex. "Oh, no, Ma'am. Not that way."

She spoke as Princess Dodu. "Oh, yes, my good man. Most definitely yes."

***

Belle and Hephaestus arrived at the town jail in Mayor Redlich's carriage. Redlich frowned as Belle fawned.

"Oh... formee-dibble," Belle said.

"Princess, I told you this wasn't such a good idea." Mayor Sam Redlich was an opportunist of the first magnitude. His wife was back east visiting relatives, which allowed him the time to enjoy the physical charms of Princess Dodu of Lorraine or whoever the hell she was. *Who knows?* he thought. *She might or might not be a real princess, but she could easily have powerful connections... could be of value to a man moving up in society. And if not... well, her charms are certainly a notch or two above those of the other women in McCloyville.* He went along with her request for a tour of his town, including his famous jail.

"I have heard of this facility in many communities." Her faux French required the use of "eet" and "faceel-ahtee." It was a corny performance, but one no one in their long journey down the California coast and then eastward through the mining towns had given a bad review. The show must, and did, go on. "You are quite famous in this land."

Redlich nodded and feigned a modest expression. When he thought she wasn't looking, he took an immodest look at her lusty figure. Belle had gained some recent weightloss on their journey. The charms and wiles of the princess combined with the hard work and illegal enterprises of Hephaestus and ShortRound had provided ample funds for rebuilding her frame.

"The prince, my father, is responsible for all the prisons in Lorraine. He would never forgive me if I did not avail myself of the opportunity to visit your American institutions."

"Well, Princess, if you can stand the smell, I can provide the tour."

"Let us begin, Monsieur."

Redlich led the princess and her faithful servant into the compound. There wasn't much to see: two adobe cells in the middle of an empty courtyard, a wooden privy set out from the wall so that it couldn't be used as a means of escape, a narrow trench from the privy lead to a grated hole in the wall, barbed wire that was even more intimidating than she'd been expecting, and a guard making a rare attempt at alertness. The moment she stepped inside, three of her five senses were assaulted: the sight was bleak and hopeless, the temperature was instantly 15 or 20 degrees hotter, and the place stunk. The heat of the sun seemed unable to make an escape. It just bounced back and forth between the walls, the buildings and the hard packed earth. She placed a perfumed handkerchief beneath her nose. Even Hephaestus choked.

"The guards say you get used to it. I don't see how," Redlich said.

"Nevertheless, Sam... Mayor Redlich... we must persevere. Come, Hephaestus."

Redlich walked them around the perimeter, approaching the privy with some trepidation. Hephaestus took particular note of the trench leading under the wall. They passed each of the cells, the one holding ShortRound last. She insisted that the doors be opened so she could get a better look at the construction.

"Oh, little persons!" She pretended a sort of delight, as if encountering a couple of Leprechauns on the heather. Belle moved quickly to examine the prisoners. While her voice said, "How precious!" her eyes said *Pay attention, you little dimwits!*

"Not too close, please, Princess. They are, after all, criminals," Redlich said.

"These little things? Mon dieu!"

"Pickpockets, Princess. A couple of experts."

"You little people really should—"

Hephaestus groaned.

She stopped and looked at him. "What is the matter?"

"I don't feel so well, Princess... my stomach. I haven't felt well all morning."

"We should leave at once and return to our lodgings," she said. Belle stood up and offered her arm to Redlich.

Hephaestus reached out and placed his arm on the wall. "With all due respect, Princess, I do not believe I have that much time."

"Explain yourself!" She was really getting into the imperial act.

"Again, respecting your every wish, my Princess, I believe a moment of privacy is imminent... if you understand my meaning, Ma'am." He moved quickly to the slop bucket in the corner.

"Oh! Mayor Redlich, thank you for the tour. Perhaps you will escort me back to my hotel?" She packed a lot of promise in her words and into the blinking of her eyes.

Redlich turned to the guard. "Watch him, then lock up." He turned and escorted the Princess away from the prison. The guard flicked his fingers on the rifle in his hands and looked at ShortRound. "You two, over in the corner. Move an inch and tonight I'll drop a whole nest of wigglers down that pipe." He looked at Hephaestus. "Do your business."

Hephaestus pulled down his britches and straddled the slop bucket. He didn't have to fake going through the motions. He'd spent a significant portion of the previous evening downing massive portions of baked beans and chili peppers.

Even the numbed senses of the guard were stunned. "You ate something that died!"

Hephaestus struggled. He grunted and groaned and sweat beads glistened on his dark skin. Several veins pulsated up his neck and into the sides of his head. At last he made a painful grunt and said, "That's it." He looked directly at ShortRound and made an embarrassed grin. "When you have to go now, you have to go now. Too bad, but that's the only way out." He looked at the guard. "Do you have any paper?"

"Paper? Hell, man, this ain't no hotel!"

"Mon dieu!" He stood up with all the mock dignity he could muster, buttoned his britches, and marched out the door. "The Princess shall hear of this!"

When the door slammed shut Short and Round stared at each other. "Did he mean what I think he meant?" Round said.

"Yeah, and he said 'now' twice. I think that's when we have to make our move—now."

"We don't even have a weapon."

"Yes we do." Short walked over to the slop bucket. "Sometimes I wish Festus wasn't such a smart son of a bitch." He reached his arm down into the warm goo and pulled out something.

"A turd?" Round gagged.

Short fought back the churning in his own belly and wiped the mess off the object by rubbing against the straw banked against a wall. The object was a cylinder about three inches in length and no more than an inch around. As Short wiped off the excrement, Round could see that the object was coated with rubber. An incision ran the circumference right in the middle. "Belle's beaver blade!'"

"Yeah, only Festus had to hide in another hole." He finished wiping it clean by rubbing it in the dirt floor. He held it up and pulled from each end to reveal a razor sharp, two-inch, double sided blade. "Now we have an edge." His eyes tightened as he ran his thumb along the edge of the blade. "And we'd better be using it tonight."

Short started a ruckus well after midnight so the guard would be less than alert. With luck he'd have been asleep or drunk and would be groggy when approaching the cell.

"What's goin' on?" the guard said. His voice was muffled by the heavy door, but even so the man's slurred words gave proof that he'd been drinking.

Good. "It's Round. He's taken ill."

"He'll keep till morning.'"

"Guard, he's really sick! He's dying!"

"Then die."

"You want that to happen on your watch?"

"Son of a bitch." A key banged against the lock several times before it was properly inserted.

"We'll stand back from the door," Short said.

"Sure, pissants." As with most men just before they are killed by their fellow man, the guard made the ultimate mistake of underestimating the cleverness, if not the size, of his enemy. The massive door swung open and the guard stepped into the darkness holding a rifle in one hand and a sputtering candle lamp in the other. "Now where's that little runt?"

Round couldn't resist a verbal answer. "Here!" He jumped on Short's shoulders, which brought him and Belle's beaver blade into close proximity to the man's jugular vein. Round leapt on the guard's back. It was a trick he and Short had played on many a drunk and many a poor whore. He made two swift slashes, one to each side of the man's neck. Both movements severed their intended targets. Round rode the dying man to the ground, his small fist stuffed in the man's mouth to muffle the weak scream that tried to escape.

Short caught the lamp and quickly blew out the light. "Move! Move! Move!" He whispered even though there was no one else in the compound. They dragged the guard from the door and dashed into the darkness. Round took time to grab the rifle and the guard's pouch of bullets.

They scrambled across the compound to the privy and stared at the narrow trench leading from it to the wall. "Like Festus said, it's the only way out. I'll go," Short said. In perhaps the bravest act of his life he slid into the trench and stopped at the iron grate. He retched twice violently before he pulled out the knife and began chiseling away at the adobe holding the bars.

Some moments later Round whispered, "My turn." He hated the thought, but he and Short shared everything, good and bad, and had done so throughout their lives. He didn't intend to welch on a contract.

"No time," Short said. He retched again. "I've... almost... got it."

Round heard a muffled grunt and the sounds of a struggle, then, "Come on!" He took a deep breath and that alone made him gag, and followed his partner, quickly adding his own vomit to that left by Short. Only one of the bars had been loosened, but it was enough. Seconds later both men were outside.

Hephaestus watched from the night shadows of a nearby building. "Here! Quick!" This was followed by a much weaker and sickly, "Christ Almighty!"

"This was your idea," Round whispered. He took only small pleasure in the faint gagging sounds from Hephaestus.

"Can we get the hell out of here?" Short said.

Hephaestus stepped into the empty road and struck a Lucifer, obviously a signal. The wind blew it out. "Damn!" He tried again and again, but the hot desert wind would not allow the flame to catch. "Just as well. The way you two smell a flame might just blow us all to hell and back. "Wait right here." He jogged off into the night.

"That's a bad start. Even the wind's against us," Short said."

Round jumped down in the dust and began rolling around like a dog. "What the hell?" Short said.

"Maybe we can rub some of this off. Or at least cover it up."

Short, seeing at least the hope of wisdom in his partner's words, joined him.

Within a moment the wagon rolled up, and Hephaestus ordered them into the rear where he'd spread a canvas tarp for them. "No use fouling up our wagon any more than required," he said. "Which way, Princess?"

Belle leaned into the wind and tried for clean air. "To the river. If we don't get these two cleaned up, the posse can track us by their stink."

"We're not too far from the Colorado. Arizona's on the other side and that's another jurisdiction."

Belle thought for a second and nodded. "You know them dire straits you mentioned?"

"Yes Ma'am."

"Well, I think we're smack dab in the middle of 'em. Better haul ass, Hephaestus."

"Yes, Ma'am!"

The wagon soon disappeared into the dark night on a lonely road to an uncertain and dangerous future. Partially dictated by the requirements of her role, but mostly dictated by then reality of the smell from the back of the wagon, Princess Dodu kept her head high and her nose in the wind all the way to the river.

LETTERS FROM
GIL CHESTERSON

I passed ten saloons on Hell Street before I stopped counting and dismounted in front of The Road to Ruin. It wasn't much of a place in a not much of a place railroad town, but I had ridden all the way from Amarillo just to receive a piece of paper. A man goes where his work takes him. The saloon was flanked by a gambling hall on the left and Annie's End of the Line on the right – a bordello. All three were constructed of green lumber and topped off with tar paper and tin. A dried pool of blood marred the east side of the saloon door. Three bullet holes right above the stain were just as bloody. I walked inside and side-stepped from the batwings to let my eyes adjust to the light.

The view didn't improve – a dirt floor, a bar that was little more than thick planks resting on a three barrels, and a small collection of unemployed cowhands already drunk. Two stared at me as if counting coins by impressions on my vest pocket. I paid them no mind as I walked to the bar. Movement from a dark corner caught my attention and my hand was half-way to my .45 Schofield when a young woman emerged and made her way straight to me.

"Gil? Is it you, Gil?" she said.

"No, Ma'am. Lee is the name, Lee Pickett."

Her face fell. She recovered quickly. "Buy me a drink?"

"Sure thing, Ma'am."

"I'm Jolene . I ain't for sale."

"Ma'am?"

"I work the saloon. I don't go in there." She nodded to a wide door leading into the bordello.

I nodded, removed my hat and shook the dust off before putting it back on. "Jolene, all I want right now is a drink and a smile."

"You got that, mister." She lost some of the tension in her body. Her smile was the freshest thing I'd seen in years. She was young, too young to be in The Road to Ruin or any other place on Hell Street. Her hair was a soft brown, her eyes a deeper brown, and she had that look that made men want to protect and at the same time possess. We talked for a while, longer than I usually talk with her kind – except Jolene wasn't "her kind."

The bartender, a fat man with a week's worth of stubble on his face showed up. "Another drink, mister?"

I looked to Jolene. "Sorry. Business."

She nodded, smiled that smile again, and walked toward the table of cowhands. Her shoulders slumped slightly with each step as if her small body was withdrawing into itself.

I spoke to the bartender. "Where can I find Clawfoot Annie?"

"Who wants to know?"

"Somebody who doesn't have a lot of patience." I used my low and mean voice. That usually scares the hell out of the easily frightened. It worked on the fat man. He stuck his head through the door to the whorehouse and then came back. "She's in the parlor. Red dress."

I walked to the end of the bar and stepped into Annie's End of the Line. The name was a perfect fit. The bordello was little more than an assembly of cribs with a roof and a central

parlor. Three women clustered around a man, most likely one of the town merchants by the way he dressed. The woman in red sat at the far end of the parlor and watched with the eyes of a hawk circling a field mouse.

"You'd be Annie?" I said.

"In the flesh." She must have weighed close to 200 pounds. Annie was attractive in her way, like one of those pictures of actresses in the newspapers. "And you'd be...."

"Pickett, Lee Pickett. I think you have a message for me."

"Sit down, Mr. Pickett, and have a drink. On the house."

She poured me a shot of whiskey. It was better than what the fat man served at the bar, not much better, but enough to show she was giving me some respect. Or maybe she was just setting me up. She said, "You've been hired to do a killing?"

"I don't talk about my business. No disrespect, Ma'am."

"None taken. But you can't blame a girl for asking questions. Here, have another drink. You got the time."

"What do you mean by that, Ma'am?"

"Call me Annie. And I mean that I'm supposed to get a telegram. I'm supposed to give that telegram to you. I am not supposed to read that telegram."

"Seems awful complicated for simple job."

"Your... our employer don't like to get his hands dirty. Or connected directly if you know what I mean."

I killed the whiskey. "Where's my telegram?"

"That's why you got time. The telegraph lines are down. Probably bronc Apaches. Won't nothing come through for a day or so. Enjoy the pleasures of Hell Street, Lee Pickett." She pointed toward her whores and then licked her lips.

"With all due respect, Alice, all I hanker for at the moment is a bath and a good steak." I tipped my hat and left. Jolene lifted her head and gave me that smile as I left the saloon.

***

Spird's Hotel was no more than a step above sleeping out on the desert sands and a short step at that. But with bronc Apaches possibly on the loose, I decided to bed down under a rat-infested roof. I slept well into the next morning, my body catching up on a lot of rough nights sleeping on rougher ground. Lunch was a sandwich at the Nameless Restaurant. That's what it was called. A walk down to the telegraph station was a waste. The lines were still down.

I went back to the Road to Ruin. Jolene seemed happy to see me. Or at least she seemed glad for an excuse to leave the company of a half-drunk drummer with clawing hands. I bought her a drink just to keep things on the up-and-up with Annie. I liked this girl. She reminded me of times long ago when I thought I'd make something of myself – back when the world was green instead of dusty brown. I worked up a question about this Gil fellow.

She said, "He's coming for me someday." She paused and looked toward the End of the Line door. "So's I don't ever have to go in there."

"What's he like?"

"I don't know, really."

The look on my face made her smile. "He writes me letters. From all over."

"But you don't know him?"

"I know it sounds funny, but he wrote he saw me one day last year. He was too fearful to buy me a drink or even to say hello. But he says, he writes, that he knew I was the only one. The 'only one.' Ain't that sweet?

I looked over to the bartender to order another couple of drinks. He rolled his eyes, but served without further comment.

"Gil writes 'bout once a month. He's out there saving his money and looking for a little ranch. He's been to Wyoming and Colorado and even California – places like that."

I just felt all warm and for a second I remembered what it was like to have a dream.

After sundown more cowhands and a lot of the business types showed up. Jolene had to move around and hustle more drinks than I could buy. I wandered into the End of the Line. Annie, sitting alone, waved me over. "Come in for some comfort, Pickett?"

"Just some company. I'm buying the liquor."

"Then I'm the company."

I felt like getting drunk, so I bought a bottle and indicated that I wanted two glasses. Annie seemed like good company – good enough for a drunk on Hell Street. She knew more about my job than I did, but not much. Some rancher down Prescott way needed to rid himself of some sheepherder. Names and all would be in the telegram.

Somewhere along the line I mumbled something about Jolene.

"Oh, she's going to be a prize, that one. The men around here will pay extra for Jolene. I'm going to see to that."

"She don't seem too keen on working this side of your building."

Annie sniffed.

"What's her story, anyway?"

Annie said, "Typical. Her family got shot all to hell between here and Winslow. She's the only one that lived. No relatives nowhere to speak of. No money. So I took her on hustling drinks. She'll be whoring soon – my best girl, I bet."

"She don't seem like the type."

"They're all the type." She helped herself to my whiskey. We were both getting fairly drunk. "This life is going to break her. Sooner or later, it's going to break her to pieces. I'll pick 'em up and put 'em to bed. I got it all mapped out."

"I wouldn't bet on it."

She laughed and waved at the fat bartender. "Ovid, bring us another bottle." She patted my knee. "You already lost."

Annie and I got drunk and talked about nothing more serious than the fools we had known. It was a long night. When I stumbled out through the bar I looked around for Jolene. I just wanted to tip my hat and say good night. She wasn't at the bar or near the tables in the back. I finally spotted her in a corner under a lamp. She was reading something. It looked like a letter. The girl seemed to be crying, so I left her alone and stumbled my way back to the rats at Spird's Hotel.

Morning came late again, but when I checked in at the telegraph, the lines were back up. The operator confirmed that a message for Clawfoot Annie had arrived earlier. I moved quickly up the street and stepped into The Road to Ruin. I looked around for Jolene, but she wasn't there. Being in a hurry I just wanted to say hello and then get on about my work. I stepped into Annie's End of the Line.

Annie sat on a couch in a corner far from the other girls. She waved me over. "Been expecting you, Pickett. Your telegram came in."

I took the envelope, took out the paper and read it. Anyone else reading the message would think it an order for certain goods to be delivered to a certain person in a certain town down south. A hired gun like me knew how to read a different message in the same words. I folded the paper and stuffed it in my pocket.

"I guess you'll be high-tailing it outta here," Annie said.

"A man's got to eat." I looked around. "Where's Jolene? I'd like to say so long."

Annie grinned. "She's in the second room. With Ovid. He wanted to be her first." She saw the stunned look on my face and her grin turned into a smile. "Like I told you, Pickett. I had it all mapped out."

"What about this Gil Chesterson fellow?"

Annie laughed. There was an evil joy in it. She leaned over. "I... I am Gil Chesterton." She laughed even louder. "Sit down and learn something." She poured two drinks. "Hair of the dog."

I sat down. The confusion I felt must have covered my face.

Annie said, "The only way I could get that girl in here was to break her. Break her spirit, break her heart. That's why I come up with this Gil Chesterton idea. I built up her hopes and dreams all year long and last night...." She stopped to laugh, almost choking on her whiskey. "Last night good old 'Gil Chesterton' wrote her that he'd found some girl in Utah and they were married and had a little ranch and were expecting children... Oh, it was a good letter."

I finished my whiskey and stood up.

She said, "You want to wait around. Ovid, he won't be long."

"Maybe when I back through this way again."

Her face got all serious and she looked hard at me. "Who you kidding, Lee Pickett?"

"Yeah. I reckon I've had enough of Hell Street."

I rode out of town, headed south. I looked back once at Clawfoot Annie's establishment, and the moved on to the more decent work of murder for hire.

Girl Fight

"**N**ekid means nekid." Chamberlain, a dirty runt employed by the town's premier whore house grinned and thumped the brim of his worn derby to punctuate his less-than-subtle advertisement.

"A bare ass girl fight?" Austin Foxworth rubbed his tongue against an incisor, action hidden by his enormous, well-greased moustache. He stared in obvious disbelief. "Not even underbritches?"

"Bare assed nekid, Mr. Foxworth."

"With guns?

"Pistols. A regular shootout."

"And *au natural*?"

"What's that mean?"

Chinese Pete approached the table. "It mean plenty nekid." He left a plate of "who-knew stew" next to Foxworth's cup of coffee, then returned with a bottle of whiskey and several shot glasses. "On house, amigos." Chinese Pete had taken to providing such extras to his dwindling list of cash customers. When the U.S. troopers and their dollars pulled out of Arizona Territory as cannon fodder for the Civil War, a steady stream of former miners, former ranchers, and former businessmen followed their example. As the Apache raids intensified, fewer and fewer of the holdouts had the time, money or inclination to patronize his Cosmopolitan Chop Shop. His wife, Chinese Mary, was out buying vegetables and preparing the restaurant's menu for the evening, so he sat down and helped himself to a shot. This surprised and flattered his customers. Chinese Pete only drank the good stuff. "Get you glasses."

"You didn't say 'grasses,' Foxworth said."

"Not in joking mood."

Chinese Pete spoke his native Mandarin, Spanish as the Mexicans speak it, and excellent English. He used pigeon English most of the time – a personal safety measure in a community where the line between the town proper and its Chinese quarter was often marked in blood. The slang also served him well when he didn't want to hear what he was hearing. "So, solly... no speak Eng-grish...." Whatever the deal, Chinese Pete tended to come out on top.

Chamberlain streaked across the floor like a tarantula on the run. He returned and handed a glass to his equally squalid partner, Arnold Lee. The scrawny little crooks hopped up on the plank seat and strained to see what came next. They killed their shots and poured a second before Chinese Pete could offer or even protest the action.

"It's for real," said Chamberlain.

"No joke," added Arnold Lee.

"I've notice attendance at Mother Damn's emporium of desire has dwindled of late," said Foxworth.

"You talk funny, Foxworth," Arnold Lee said.

Chinese Pete grabbed his bottle. "He say, not many customers whore house, *Ladron*."

Chamberlain, knowing a tiny bit of Spanish, took offense at being called "thief," but he smiled and extended his arm for more good whiskey.

"Chamberlain, Arnold Lee, I feel you are spreading a *sugestio falsi*, my boys." The banker never tired of slinging fancy words and expressions at the town's most obvious and least successful thieves. He told one of his banking customers, "I love to watch that wave of confusion cross their squinty faces. It's like a parade flag caught in a breeze."

"Mother Damn, she calls it a reckoning," Chamberlain said.

In fits and starts and quick grabs at Chinese Pete's bottle of booze, Chamberlain and Arnold Lee spilled the story. Some madam from a big whorehouse back east was passing through on her way to California. She and Mother Damn didn't exactly gee and haw in tandem back in the old days, and there had been real trouble over men and money down in New Orleans. When Mother Damn left for the West she vowed to someday even up whatever score needed to be settled. Chamberlain wasn't exactly full of details. He said Mother Damn had gotten wind of the woman's travel plans and had "called her out," the note having been carried on one of the last stages before Butterfield Overland pulled out of Arizona.

Foxworth plopped down a few coins more than required for the stew. "The next round is on me, Pete. This sounds like one of Mother Damn's stunts."

"Si, es verdad. People need eat now. They do not need whore." Chinese Pete spoke as one successful business man to another, as if discussing a marketing plan.

"Well, I haven't noticed you making any contributions to Mother's coffers. Fact is, you've been rather scarce since you and Mary tied the knot sublime."

Chinese Pete was stung by Foxworth's comment, mostly because it was true. Chinese Mary kept her man on a short leash. "Save money. Get out of Arizona muy pronto. Apache coming soon," she say. And she say it often."

Chamberlain looked at Foxworth. "You're gonna be there, ain't ya'?"

Foxworth killed his drink, patted Chinese Pete on the shoulder and stood up. The prayer meeting was over. He looked at Chamberlain and Arnold Lee. "Run tell Mother Damn that the good banker Foxworth remains an aficionado of her ever-expanding repertoire." Again he enjoyed the flag of confusion that rippled across two dirty faces.

"He show up. Now you go." Chinese Pete stood up and collected the dishes as the two dirty thieves scampered out the door to further spread the good word. "Pete, Mother Damn's going to have one hell of an audience. But even naked as a jaybird, I'll be damned if I can see how she's going to make a dime out of a free show."

"Ask Chamberlain. Ask Arnold Lee."

"My life would be blessed should I never encounter that pair again."

Chinese Pete dumped the dishes in a tub of water. "You better see Arnold Lee plenty soon, amigo."

"In God's name why?"

"He steal your watch."

Foxworth stomped away without so much as a confirming touch to his empty watch pocket. It had happened before.

***

Two weeks after Foxworth had retrieved his watch he and Chinese Pete stood in front of the restaurant anticipating the big showdown. Chinese Pete continually looked over his shoulder, trying to ignore the banging, clanging, rattling of dishes and occasional oriental curse words fired from inside. Not only was the Chinaman about to get an eyeful in front of his restaurant, he was also assured an earful for much of the foreseeable future from within.

Foxworth arrived with a friendly greeting and a bottle of good whiskey insisting that that Chinese Pete produce shot glasses. "Drinking such nectar from a bottle is sacrilege," he said. The banker did not share the common prejudice against the Chinese found in many other western towns. Chinese Pete was not only one of his best customers, but a trusted friend.

Just as Chinese Pete arrived with the glassware they heard the unmistakable, ominous buzz of a large rattlesnake. Acting upon instinct as old as mankind each jumped into the street. Foxworth reached for his pistol. He turned to face a giggling 12 year old Davy Fontaine gleefully shaking the rattles he'd taken from the previous owner some time back. He said he carried them as a good luck charm, but the charm was more often used to perpetrate this very stunt.

"Damn it, Davy!"

"Malcontento!" added Chinese Pete.

Davy just laughed. "When does the fun begin?"

Foxworth glanced at his pocket watch. "I give 'er about another half-hour."

"You got program, amigo?" asked Chinese Pete.

"Nah. I just figure that'll give Mother Damn about enough time to work up an audience."

"You think this is all about money, Mr. Foxworth," Davy said."

"*Esta bean correcto*. Mother Damn alla time making money," Pete said.

Of course, Foxworth thought. "Gentlemen, to all but the most dense or willingly self-deluded, which described most of the population now lining our main street, this event has to be a scheme. But how the hell is Mother Damn going to squeeze money from a free-show," he said.

That this was a well-planned stunt was of no doubt. The coincidences piled up like the dusty tailings at one of now deserted silver mines. A former enemy from Mother Damn's mysterious past just happens to be traveling through the territory. Word of the woman's travels just happens to filter out ahead of her visit. No one knew the source, but the pony express riders carrying the word were always named Chamberlain and Arnold Lee. That Mother Damn had sent a challenge and that the challenge had been received and accepted also defied common sense. And then there was the challenge itself: a bare-assed gunfight between two women. Clearly, the object was to drum up as big an audience of horny men as possible, a scheme that had worked amazingly well. Half the population of south-central Arizona lined the dusty street.

"No clothes," Pete said.

"*In puris naturalibus*," Foxworth said.

"Butt-by-God nekid!" added Davy.

Another metal plate hit the floor inside the restaurant.

Footsteps on the wooden sidewalk announced the arrival of a new spectator. The deep Southern accent flowed like a Louisiana bayou in summer, languid and with barely a ripple of emphasis when he said, "Excuse me, gentlemen, but what time does this affair begin? Marcus Antonius Noye, at your service."

"Stewart Foxworth. This is Chinese Pete. The boy is Davy."

"Pleased to meet you, gentlemen." He shook each hand, even Chinese Pete's. "A curious town you have here. And curious amusement."

The voice did not sound out of place. Unlike the western portion of New Mexico Territory, Arizona was full of southerners. The man's suit gave him away as a newcomer. It was clean—dusty, but clean. He was as lanky as a willow. He wore a dress suit and vest, carried a silk handkerchief, and a dark derby cocked at a confident angle over a full head of curly brown hair. He was unarmed, another clue that he was from other parts. Instead of a pistol or a shotgun he carried a leather bound notebook and pencil. "I'm a reporter from New Orleans. Gathering western views on the coming war."

"The war should stay in the East where it belongs. I say let the South go its own way... just as we do."

Noye agreed. "If the South wants to leave the party, I say let them depart. There's plenty of this country to go around."

Davy spoke up. "We already got lots o' war, Mister."

The comment caught Foxworth off guard. He'd never thought of the situation in that light. Between the Indians, the bandits and killers the territory certainly was at war and a damned bloody one at that. He made a mental note to keep a closer watch on young LaFontaine. The boy showed promise of clear thinking, a rare commodity. For the moment, however, he was more interested in divining information from the recent arrival. "Pete, would you consider another glass for our newfound friend?"

"I am honored, gentlemen," said Noye.

The Chinaman dashed inside, returning glass in hand in a move even more swiftly. "Show start plenty fast!" All thoughts of drinking were forgotten as Chinese Pete pointed toward the far end of town.

A wagon guarded by two tough-looking riders rolled into view. Next to the equally tough-looking driver sat a petite woman covered neck to toe in a red blanket. The Queen of Sheba could not have looked more regal. Or more out of place. Her small nose was tilted up in a show of disdain for her audience, or perhaps she was just trying to sniff some clean air. Her hair was curly blonde and even from a distance, they could see that her eyes were deep blue. Heavy makeup made her look even more exotic. A miner pretended to faint in ecstasy and fell into the dirt. His two partners believed the act and stepped on his body for a better look at the parade. The object of their attention paid the ruckus no mind.

"Her name is Delta," Noye said.

Foxworth looked at him. "You know her?"

"Rode up with the party from Tucson a few days ago. Thought I'd come in early to get a seat for the show."

Foxworth slapped his hands together. "I knew it! This whole shebang is a farce, isn't it?" He loved being proven right even when he was a step or two behind everyone else's recognition of the obvious.

"Mother Damn is always figurin' out new ways to make money," Davy said.

Foxworth grinned. "I still wonder how the hell she's going to turn this open-air display into hard currency."

Chinese Pete shouted, "There! Mother Damn."

The true queen of the town arrived at last. She sat high and mighty in her fancy carriage, which was driven by one of her whores. Mother Damn sported a red blanket. The carriage was driven closer until the carriage and the wagon carrying two women in red were about 25 yards apart. Mother Damn stepped down and had her trademark "accident" with the blanket, briefly exposing one of her ample breasts. The crowd laughed and hooted as she pretended to ignore them.

Foxworth watched as a couple of men eased out of the Armageddon Saloon and made their way behind the crowd up toward Mother Damn's place of business. Each man carried a box filled with whiskey bottles. The tinkling of the glass was the sound of money. His smile grew broader.

The attractive newcomer waited for her moment. When the rude chatter stopped and all eyes turned her direction, she glanced at one of her riders. The man climbed down from his horse and offered his arm. Like a fair damsel in a storybook tale, she stepped down. Several men cheered. She nodded gracefully in their direction.

Noye nodded. "Nice touch, that."

Delta let the red blanket slide from her shoulders. It seemed to melt down her skin and puddle at her feet. All the cheering stopped as a street full of lonely men collectively gasped for air. She was perfectly formed, her golden hair piled along the perfect, pale skin of her shoulders. Her legs slightly apart, her stance was defiant.

Mother Damn marched down the street, stopping a pace or so from her small enemy. She slung her blanket to the dirt in a move that made up for a lack of grace with sheer power. Her large body was beginning to fade, but deep into the woman-starved territory the lines and creases of age were obliterated by pure horniness. Mother

Damn always knew how to whip up a crowd, and this time she'd outdone her own considerable talents.

"Damnation!" Davy said.

"I thought this was a gunfight." Foxworth's voice was a whisper.

Noye shook his head. "Too much chance of an accident. That was just a... fabrication... to drum up more interest, you see." Neither man took his eyes from the scene being played out on the dusty street. "Besides, there's something more...." The journalist searched for the correct word. "*Arresting* about two nude women going bare-knuckle, so to speak."

The women met in one of the few areas of the street absent horse or mule dung. Mother Damn spread her legs, closed her fists and prepared to hammer her opponent into the ground. "I've been waiting a long time for this, you harelequin!" she said.

Foxworth leaned over to Chinese Pete. "This thing's been plotted out better than a novel from Fennimore Cooper."

Delta jerked her head, nose to the air. "You'll rue the day you ever set eyes on me, Mother-be-damned."

Foxworth grimaced. "Dialog's not much better, either."

Noye bowed his head ever so slightly. "Sir, you have just offended the author."

Foxworth returned the bow with a slight nod. "I see. Well, Sir, you have earned an apology." He poured another round of drinks. Both men chuckled.

Noye said, "A writer must earn his keep and journalism pays so poorly."

"Don't quite seem fair. Mother Damn is a whole person bigger than that lady," Davy said.

"Free will, my boy. Nothing could be more fair than that," Foxworth said.

Noye dragged his eyes from the street scene and saw something in Davy's eyes that he had seen very little of out West. *The kid is actually worried about the little lady out in the street,* he thought. The reporter squatted down and offered his glass to the young man. "Take a sip and prepare to be educated about the ways of your fellow man."

Davy, already an experienced drinker, swallowed the whiskey in a single gulp.

Noye patted him on the back. "This is nothing more than a stage show, young man—planned, plotted, negotiated and choreographed for the entertainment of the masses." The sound of fair flesh hitting fair flesh caught their attention. Both men stood up.

Mother Damn and Delta were taking wild swings at each other. Few actually connected and when they did the blows created more noise than harm. Still, the crowd cheered. Bets were made and money changed hands. While the petite new arrival was by far the emotional favorite, all the smart money was on the larger, more powerful Mother Damn.

A swing and a miss from Mother Damn opened an opportunity and Delta grabbed it—rather, she grabbed her opponent. She lunged under the large woman's arms and tackled her, and both women fell into the dusty street. They rolled back and forth, neither gaining an advantage over the other. Each punched, slapped and pulled the hair of her opponent. Foxworth noted that Mother Damn never really exploited her overwhelming advantage in size and strength.

Davy, now "educated" to the wiles of mankind, noted something else. In every fight between man, woman, child and animal he'd ever seen there was always a considerable amount of biting. This struggle was surely different. Neither Mother Damn nor Delta drew first blood. They rolled and screamed and slapped with no sign of a clear winner. If there was more noise than fight the crowd of lonely men didn't mind one bit.

Inevitably, Mother Damn began to get the better of her opponent. The cheers of "fight on, Li'l Lady" for her smaller opponent filled her with an evil fury, or so it appeared.

One of the miners said, "Ol' Mother Damn don't cotton to nobody steppin' in her spotlight, do she?"

Delta bobbed and weaved to avoid the blows from Mother Damn's large arms. She dodged and ducked like a professional, all the time looking for another opening. Both were winded, but Banker Foxworth thought that all the breast heaving was a bit exaggerated. Mother Damn took another swing, but missed. As before, the diminutive Delta used the opportunity to move in close. But this time Mother Damn was ready and scooped up the smaller woman like a sack of potatoes. She screamed as Mother Damn lifted her off her feet. An audible sigh of regret filtered through the crowd. The show was about over.

"I fear you shall kill me, Mother Damn!"

"And kill you I shall, Harlot!"

Foxworth leaned toward Noye. "Is this a fair representation of your writing style, Marcus Antonius Noye?"

Noye grinned. "My benefactor—she must remain nameless, you see—insisted that I make the dialog 'dayum faincee.'"

Delta screamed again and seemed to faint. Mother Damn dropped the small woman to the street. The fall must have pulled her back to consciousness, for she began to back away from her larger antagonist. Her feet kicked at the dirt as she scrambled back. Stark terror did not prevent her from skillfully avoiding a pile of horse manure in the dirt.

A miner at the edge of the street voiced the question floating through the crowd. "You ain't really gonna kill 'er, are you?"

"I shall send her to the fiery pits!" Mother Damn's fierce look halted a couple of miners tentatively moving toward her victim. Chamberlain and Arnold Lee popped into the streets, each holding a sawed-off shotgun. Nobody moved except Mother Damn.

Davy stood up. "She can't do that!" He moved as if about to dash into the street, tackle Mother Damn and give the poor newcomer a chance to run for her life. Provided he could escape the larger woman's clutches, he planned to follow her example as quickly as possible. Noye grabbed him by the shoulder. "Observe and learn, young man."

Chinese Pete poured himself, Foxworth and Noye another shot of whiskey. Davy sneaked the bottle and poured himself shot. Mother Damn stalked toward Delta and quickly straddled the small woman. "The means of her destruction, Chamberlain," she said.

Chamberlain backed further into the street and handed the weapon over.

Mother Damn spoke to Delta, but she looked to the men. "Your tawdry features shall no longer blemish this fair land!"

Foxworth swallowed a laugh. "Noye!"

"Please, Sir, drivel though it may be, it is having the desired effect."

True enough. Every miner, ranch hand, citizen and trail bum in town seemed to believe the unbelievable scene unfolding before their eyes. Noye patted Davy on his shoulder. "Never underestimate the human ability for self-delusion."

Davy sat down, shaking his head.

"What the hell is she going to do next?" Foxworth scratched his chin.

Mother Damn cocked both barrels of the shotgun and took aim at the woman beneath her feet.

"Mother Damn, wait!"

"I'd rather go to hell myself!" Mother Damn said.

"Dropped a line there," whispered Noye.

Delta shook her head as if confused, but then continued. "Spare me!"

Mother Damn picked up her cue. "I'd rather go to hell myself!"

"Then grant me one boon before I die."

Foxworth giggled. "Boon?"

"I was short of words and out of time," Noye said.

Mother Damn pointed the shotgun into the air. "All right, I shall grant you a wish before you die. Name it."

"I've never had a man. I am... a virgin!"

Foxworth and Chinese Pete dropped their glasses. One hit Davy on the head. Chinese Pete took a swig directly from the bottle and handed it to Foxworth, who did the same and passed it on to Noye, who followed the example and then passed it to Davy. "I think you'll appreciate the final touches," Noye said.

Mother Damn handed the shotgun to Chamberlain. He uncocked it and lowered the barrel toward the street. Arnold Lee stood nearby. Mother Damn picked up Delta, walked across the street and dumped her in a water trough. As Arnold Lee handed Mother Damn her blanket, Delta stood up and shook her head. As if choreographed, which in a way they certainly were, the men slowly formed a circle around the woman.

Davy said, "She's sparkling!" As small drops of water, collecting the rays of the sun, sparkled down her fair skin, she shook her head and began straightening her hair. The men were stunned.

Mother Damn's jealous side bristled with anger, but her business side cackled with delight.

Mother Damn stepped up beside the trough. "What is my bid?"

Her answer was silence.

"For sale, one virgin bride to the highest bidder. The sale is to begin shortly at Mother Damn's House of Mirrors."

Arnold Lee helped Delta step from the trough. Mother Damn led the party up the street toward the whore house. None of the men moved as all eyes followed the bouncing curves of Delta's delightful bottom.

Foxworth, Noye and Chinese Pete joined Davy in the swirling dust. The bottle made its way back and forth again. "I'll be damned!" said Foxworth. "She going to auction off a whore!"

"Mother Damn smart businesswoman. Plenty smart," Pete said.

"She's going to clean out every son of a bitch in town," Foxworth said.

"But there's only one Miss Delta," Davy said.

Foxworth chuckled. "And there's lots of whores and lots of time at the House of Mirrors tonight."

Noye spoke with authority. "Mother Damn and Delta have done this before. In the back streets of Natchez, New

Orleans and a few other places. This is the first time they've done it out West, I believe. Of course, that's not for print. You boys coming to the party?"

The loud "smack" of a metal plate on a table top provided the answer for Chinese Pete.

"I think Mary has your plans for the evening already mapped out," said Foxworth. "I, on the other hand, would be delighted to escort a member of the press to our community's most fashionable establishment."

With the streets clear and the sunlight scattering in the late afternoon sun, Davy Fontaine sat alone in front of Chinese Pete's restaurant. The mysteries of Mother Damn, Delta and their activities at the House of Mirrors would remain mysteries for a while. For the moment, he had a bottle of good whiskey in hand and the rest of the night to ponder the curious ways of the West.

— THE END —

About the Author

Dan Baldwin is the author of the westerns Bock's Canyon, Trapp Canyon, A Stalking Death, Caldera, Caldera-A Man on Fire, and Caldera-A Man of Blood; the mysteries Desecration, Heresy and Vengeance; the thriller Sparky and the King and two short story collections, Vampire Bimbos on Spring Break and Dank Summit and Other Stories, and the photo book series Wildflower Stew. He is the winner of numerous local, regional, and national awards for writing and directing film and video projects. He earned an Honorable Mention from the Society of Southwestern Authors writing competition for his short story Flat Busted and earned a Finalist designation from the National Indie Excellence Awards for Trapp Canyon and for Caldera III – A Man of Blood and a Finalist designation in the New Mexico-Arizona Book Awards for Sparky and the King. His They Are Not Yet Lost non-fiction work on psychic detecting earned the Winner designation in the New Mexico-Arizona Book Awards Competition. He is the ghostwriter or co-author of more than 60 books on business. Baldwin is a resident of Phoenix-Mesa, Arizona.

Books By Dan Baldwin

Non-Fiction
FIND ME as told to Dan Baldwin
How FIND ME Lost Me
The Practical Pendulum – Getting into the Swing of Things
They Are Not Yet Lost – True Stories of Psychic Detecting
Speaking With Spirits of the Old Southwest by Dan Baldwin and
    Dwight and Rhonda Hull
Just the FAQs About Alcohol and Drug Abuse (with George Sewell)
The Levine Project (with Myles and Karen Levine)

Novels
Caldera
Caldera-A Man on Fire
Caldera – A Man of Blood
Bock's Canyon
Trapp Canyon
Sparky and the King-The Plot to Assassinate Elvis Presley
Desecration (An Ashley Hayes mystery)
Heresy (An Ashley Hayes mystery)
Vengeance (An Ashley Hayes Mystery)
A Stalking Death

Novellas/Short Story Collections
Vampire Bimbos on Spring Break
Dank Summit and Other Short Stories
Jimi Strawberry's Gas Bomb and More Stories from Dank Summit
Gila River Trails and Other Western Stories

Photo Books
Wildfire Stew #1
Wildfire Stew #2 – Bugs 'n Bees
Wildfire Stew #3 – More Bloomin' Arizona
Wildfire Stew #4 – The Whole Bunch
*Wildflower Stew # 5 – Gila Sunrise – Stirring Things Up in New
    Mexico*

All of Dan Baldwin's books are available in paperback and e-book formats from Amazon, CreateSpace, Smashwords, B&N and all major distributors.

Contact Dan at:

baldco@msn.com

www.fourknightspress.com

www.danbaldwin.biz

If You Liked...

If you Gila River Trails Western Short Story Collection, you will probably also like:

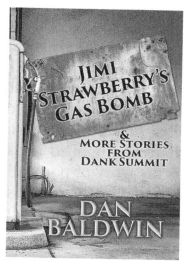

Jim Strawberry's Gas Bomb
& More Stories from Dank Summit

~~Excerpt~~

Jimi Strawberry's Gas Bomb

Jimi Strawberry woke up and crawled out of the rolling waves submerged in his king-sized waterbed. He rolled over the hand-varnished 2x12 mahogany bedframe, stretched and did a few squats to jumpstart the old heartbeat. The crackling of his knee joints sounded like a young war kicking off on the other side of the hill. He looked in the mirror and grasped the dresser with both hands.

"You're either on the bus or off the bus." He winked and smiled.

He stepped into the shower, sprayed his body and quickly turned off the water. He lathered up with organic soap blissfully hand made by his girlfriend, Melanie Clover Meadowfield. The soap smelled like a mix of roses and rotgut, but a gift is a gift especially if hand delivered by an attractive sixties throwback who pretended to know what 'you're either on the bus or off the bus' means. Melanie had a good heart and talented hands, but she wasn't the brightest bubble in the lava lamp. Swathed in suds, he ran the water just enough to de-lather before stepping from the stall. After drying off on his genuine hemp towels he combed his gray hair and opened the top drawer of his dresser. Inside was an array of ponytail bands. Each one was made of hand-tooled leather embossed with mantras important to Jimi and his generation. He had them arranged by days.

Give peace a chance Monday.
Make love not war Tuesday.
Peace! Wednesday.
Power to the People Thursday.
Go with the flow Friday.
Outtasight Saturday.
Dorothy Provine Sunday.

He selected one of his favorite anyday bands – Right On! - and locked it in place just behind his occipital bump. His hair reflected his outlook on life that day – straight and tight up front for the squares, but, like Jimi, loose and free behind the image. Looking again into the mirror he said, "If you're not part of the solution, you're part of the problem."

His '68 VW van nestled in his three-car garage was like a second home and he approached it with a reverence one gives a holy relic. It had been rebuilt from the ground up and was on its second engine, but from the looks of the exterior the vehicle could have just pulled out of a Viet Nam War protest. The original flower-power art and protest slogans had long worn away. But a few years back he hired an artist to replicate the original in shiny and permanent paint.

As he drove downhill toward central Dank Summit he glanced back at his home. "The castle" was built by his great-grandfather. The old boy had been a roughneck in the Louisiana oilpatch who had the incredible good fortune to have an ace up his sleeve in a card game late one night in some long-forgotten back-bayou whiskey bar. The ace won him a hole in the ground in the middle of a mass of red dirt that came to be known as the Rodessa Field, one of the richest oil deposits in the United States. The old roughneck became staggeringly wealthy and he wanted to make a permanent statement to that effect. He built the castle to look like the one in the Frankenstein and Dracula films of the thirties. It was big, gray and imposing, just like the old man. Although Jimi loudly and often denounced the industry from which his fortune grew, he loved the stone fortress, especially on Halloween when he turned it into a playhouse for Dank Summit's little monsters.

His mind blew back to the moment that set this day in motion, a meeting with his banker several weeks earlier.

Xavier Hollander was a middle-aged bank manager and Mr. Drysdale to Jimi's Jed Clampett. His primary concern was trying to keep the substantial Jimi Strawberry trust fund intact. And in the bank. He flopped back in his leather seat and wiped his hand across his comb-over. "You want a gas station!"

Jimi said, "A *service* station."

"Jimi, are you possessed? You're a dadblamed socialist."

"Capitalistic socialism – it's the wave of the future. Catch it, Xavier."

"You *are* possessed."

"I want a service station that provides ultra-service, something new for the people."

"*The people* want cheap gas and a place to buy cold beer and potato chips."

"I know what the people want. And I'm going to see that they get it. Service beyond service. Horsepower to the people."

Hollander couldn't talk Jimi out of his latest fantasy, so the money was allocated for the project and within a month the citizens of Dank Summit were buzzing about the new enterprise. Jimi bought an existing station and began making improvements immediately. A sign went up the first day.

It's A Gas!
Turn in! Tune Up!
Go Where No Station Has Gone Before!
(A Strawberry Feels Co.)

– Excerpt from *Jim Strawberry's Gas Bomb & More Stories from Dank Summit*

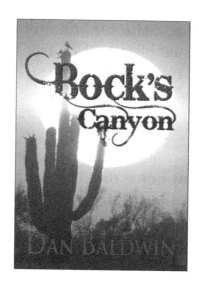

Bock's Canyon

~~Excerpt~~

Part One
Brodie

Chapter 1

"You goin' up against a .44 with just a pen knife, kid?"

"It's all I got."

"It ain't enough."

The kid screamed and rushed the big man. His small knife cut into the man's heavy coat, but never struck muscle or even flesh. A second later he was sprawled across his father's body on the packed dirt floor of their small cabin. Jocko Henderson looked down on the pitiful sight. "You got more sand than your daddy, boy. Don't let it get you killed."

"Leave my mama alone!"

Tule Henderson, a shorter and more compact version of his brother, turned his attention from the woman. "Kill that little bastard. He's crampin' my style."

"Shut up, Tule."

The woman pleaded. "Don't hurt my boy. Please don't...."

Tule slapped her across the face. He ripped the top of her dress and threw her across the room onto a bed made of rough-cut wood. "Me first, Jocko."

"Take your time." Jocko pulled a twist of tobacco and took a bite.

Tule crossed the room, watching with a smile as the woman crawled back on the worn blankets. "I'm carrying a child. Please...."

"You're going to be carrying a lot more 'n that, lady."

Tule dropped his suspenders, threw his stained felt hat to the floor and crawled on the bed. "Let's see what you got to show me." He grabbed her dress with a laugh.

The boy jumped up, his hands red with his father's blood, but Jocko easily grabbed him by the neck and threw him against the wall. "I ought to kill you right now, boy."

The kid steadied himself against the wall. "You better."

Jocko laughed.

The woman screamed.

The kid made another rush, his screams drowning those of his mother. Jocko caught him by the throat again, dragged him across the room and shoved him against the small woodstove in the corner of the one-room cabin. The iron was still hot from the morning's meal, but the pain of seeing what Tule was doing to his mother drove away the pain of the hot metal.

"Don't hurt her no more!"

"Woman was born to hurt, boy. Don't you know that?" Jocko held the boy to the stove with one hand and scratched his privates with the other. "Now, you watch and learn."

Tule had mounted the woman, holding his hand over her mouth to shut out her screams. The kid looked away. Jocko moved quickly and held the boy's head between his hands, forcing him to watch. "Look!"

When Tule finished, Jocko took his turn and Jocko was a rough man. Tule, like his brother, held the boy's head so that he was forced to watch.

Tule shoved a torn rag in the kid's mouth to stop his shouting. He sat down on a bench against the wall and watched his brother at work.

The kid struggled and wept.

When Jocko finished, he stood up and buttoned his britches. He looked down at the woman and grunted. He strapped on his belt. "Let's go."

Tule stood up. "I want me one more time."

"No, you don't."

"And why not big brother?"

"She's dead."

The kid, no longer screaming, no longer weeping, just stared at Jocko.

"You better kill that boy while you can, big brother."

Jocko laughed. "I like him. But, you're right."

– Excerpt from ***Bock's Canyon***

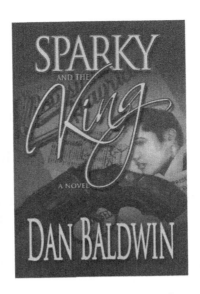

Sparky and the King

~~Excerpt~~

Chapter 1

"Fer Chrissakes, Jack, you're getting blood on the customers!"

Jack Ruby's grasp on the drunk's collar tightened as his target struggled to get off the carpeted floor of the night club. The victim's heels kicked and slipped and he reached back to support himself for the inevitable next blow. Jack, straddling his prey, struck his customer once more in the face, letting go of his grip at the same time. The back of the guy's head hit the floor with the sound of a watermelon striking pavement. Jack backed away and started to straighten his hair, stopping in mid-motion because of the blood on his hands.

Harwood, a dark-haired young man just slightly wider than his thin black tie tugged on his boss's jacket and eased him back toward the stage. The stripper a few feet above and behind them had stopped her gyrations. The small band had stopped playing. The customers had stopped drinking and were gawking at the incident. "Why'd you hit him in front of the customers, Jack?"

Jack sneered. "To show the son of a bitch Jews have guts."

The stripper on stage, Jaylene Joy, backed away from the corner of the stage and raised her gown carefully to avoid the blood spots that had splattered her forward dancing area. She shook her head and snorted at the condition of the man who was gaining an unwanted and intimate knowledge of the spilled beer and cigarette butts littering the floor. She stepped past the emcee, who did his own eclectic dance to the microphone.

He grinned, waved his arms and imitated a circus clown clapping his hands. "All part of the show folks, all part of the show." He snapped his fingers toward the bartender and the room went dark except for the stage. He snapped again and the five-piece band broke into an ill-rehearsed version of "Yellow Polka Dot Bikini," a Top 40 hit from a year or so back.

Jaylene backed through the curtains as Jack wiped the blood off his brass knuckles. A man and a woman at a nearby table stood up and backed away. Two men at another table eased their chairs back, but did not get up. The smiles on their faces showed anticipation of more of "the show."

The man with the bloody face turned over and grabbed the wide center pole that supported his table. He tried to pull himself up, but Jack kicked him in the butt, the grabbed him by the belt and dragged him to the front door. Harwood tried to help, but Jack just shoved him aside.

The drummer crafted a five second roll on his snare and finished with a rim shot. As the crowd looked from Jack to the stage, the emcee grinned more broadly. "Like I said, folks, it's all part of the show at Jack Ruby's Carousel Club. And as a special welcome and a friendly hello from the management of Dallas' premier burlesque club, one shot of whatever you're having is on the house!"

Jack cursed beneath at the cheers of the audience. They were mostly working folk, hack lawyers, bored salesmen and a few regulars. All were happy to ignore the violence for a shot of Jack's cheap booze. They would notice him only briefly, if at all, as he dragged his half-conscious victim across the floor. The regulars smiled and shook their heads as if seeing a repeat performance of an earlier event. The way most of the others were either shouting drink orders or ogling Jaylene as she sashayed back onto the stage showed they didn't give a rat's ass about Jack's victim.

Harwood moved behind the bar to help with the sudden influx of orders. The band kicked in with a bouncy tune and Jaylene, even more bouncy, stepped back into her spotlight.

The poor dumb sap in Jack's grasp had fallen prey to his own vanity and had made two mistakes. His first was an attempt to show off by buying one of the B-Girls a couple of bottles of exorbitantly priced cheap champagne. His second was getting drunk. His drinking partner, Raynelle, didn't, and that only made him drink harder to prove that he was a "drinkin' man." He never saw her dumping most of her booze into the white towel covering the ice bucket containing each bottle. Raynelle was a pro. She didn't get drunk because she didn't drink heavily with the customers.

Jack knew the guy, a loser named Griffen. His application for work had been shot down a few years earlier by the Dallas Police Department, an organization not known for discriminating recruitment policies. Since half the cops in Dallas hung out at the Carousel, the bum felt he was due special privileges as a brother in arms. Griffen worked as a night watchman at some currently-unwatched building down the street. Only a few cops considered him a brother in arms, and then only when he was drunk enough to buy a round or two.

Griffen pushed his luck when he pushed Raynelle for a little action. When his voice had drawn attention from Jaylene's performance, Jack had stepped in. His manicured fingers dug into Griffen's shoulder. He spoke quietly, but his eyes were those of a bird of prey. "Why don't you go on home and pile up some Zs? I'll call you a cab."

Raynelle backed up in her chair.

Jack was short and appeared to be pudgy, a misleading image. He worked out regularly at an athletic club and was far stronger than he looked—far meaner, too.

The drunk night watchman pointed his index finger at Raynelle. "This bitch of yours is soaking me, Ruby."

"Sir, we do not have bitches and we do not soak our clientele." Jack's jaw tightened. *Bitch got caught soaking another sucker. She's history.*

"Three bottles of champagne I bought her."

"We appreciate your patronage."

"An' she don't come around."

"The Carousel is a class act, Sir. Nobody 'comes around.' "

"Class my ass." He giggled and straightened out his face. "I know all about you and your damn kosher nostra,

Ruby. You'd sell out your mamma for a couple of bucks." He stuck out his jaw. The drunk meant it as a challenge. Jack saw it as an opportunity.

If Griffen had really known his host he would have known about the man's temper. Raynelle backed farther away and by the time she stood up Jack was using his brass knuckles to relocate Griffen's nose. Jack was powerful and fast, and the fight, such as it was, never left the table until he dragged away the instigator of the brawl. That had been less than a minute earlier and now the guy was halfway out the door.

Jack kicked him in the butt and the man crawled into the stairwell. Jack kicked again and Griffen rolled down to the first floor. As Jack followed him he smelled the iron-rich blood on his fists. It mingled with the aromas from the first floor delicatessen. He took a deep breath and licked his lips. All his senses were active and alive.

Griffen's roll down the stairs had created a few new cuts and scrapes. Blood from his head wounds dripped on the concrete sidewalk as he crawled onto Commerce Street and gazed at the lights from the fashionable Hotel Adolphus across the street. Jack often said being so close to a Dallas landmark gave his club class. No one was on the street. Only a few cars were moving and they were a couple of blocks away. "No more, Ruby... please."

"Kosher Nostra, eh?" Jack bent over and punched the man in the mouth. "Maybe when you get your new teeth I'll take you on as a comic."

"No. Jack, I won't—"

Jack helped him to his feet. "Know what a punch line is, prick?" Jack rammed his fist into Griffen's gut, dropping him again. The man rolled over and puked Jack's cheap booze, then followed it with a blood chaser. He got up on all fours only to be dropped again by a powerful kick to the kidneys. Jack put his foot on the man's neck, rubbing his face in his own blood and vomit.

Griffen looked up Commerce Street and the shredded flesh that had been his lips formed a half-smile as a Dallas PD patrol car came around the corner. The vehicle slowed and stopped in front of the Carousel. Two policemen stepped out.

The driver spoke with a broad grin on his face. "Got a little trouble there, Jack?"

"Nothing I can't handle."

"Well, handle it inside, okay?"

– Excerpt from *Sparky and the King*

Vampire Bimbo's ...on Spring Break

~~Excerpt~~

Chapter One

The vampire had one hell of an aching, hacking, coughing, itching, aching, can't sleep at night, snot-slinging head cold - a common side effect of chowing down on the blood of an afflicted victim. His full name was Bojangles Osiris Bahr-Isuf, but since the turn of the latest century those who knew him called him Bob, a mysterious and wealthy member of New York's most remarkable nightlife. Through the ages far beyond the murky dawn of history he had been a shaman, a wizard, a wealthy industrialist, a baron, a Templar knight *and* a Saracen prince, and a number of men of true power, prestige and presence.

"Wah-chew!"

The fellow shopper at the corner If I Ain't Got It You Don't Need It Store backed away.

"Jeeze, Mister! You ate something that died."

Bob shrugged off criticism and continued looking through the cold remedy section for a medicine he knew did not exist.

"I mean they oughta' hand out nasal blocker around you," the man said.

The vampire tried to ignore the ugly customer, but he wouldn't stop. "Mister, you really reek. What do you brush with? A dead beaver?"

Bob turned and stared into the boob's eyes. The man froze in his steps and his eyes glazed over. "Take a deep breath." He slowly blew a deep and slow blast of fetid air in the man's face. "That's it. Take it all in." When his fellow shopper turned the appropriate shade of green Bob puffed a final blast and walked away. As he left the building he saw the man spraying himself with an aerosol can of I Can't Believe It Don't Stink No More. Judging from the way the other shoppers quickly edged away, he was the victim of another case of false advertising.

Bob's breath was just a byproduct of being a member of the lonely fraternity of the undead. A few decades earlier he'd tried brushing his teeth, mouthwashes, and gargling all to no avail. He had even received regular thank-you-for-your-bulk-order notes from Altoids and Listerine. When he went out - nights only, of course - he favored restaurants featuring spicy dishes to cover the odor. Heavy tipping and incredible charm helped, too

The night was cold, miserable and wet and so was Bob. A savage wind drove the icy rain right through his heavy cape and business suit right down to what that Borgia woman used to call his "poo poo undies." He looked through the window of Larissa's Tofu-4-U Restaurant and shook his head. *To hell with bean curd. Vampires need meat - juicy, blood-red meat.*

A woman wearing granny glasses who couldn't see that the sixties had faded with her youthful dreams stretched and arched her back to expose a long, slender and hickey-laminated neck – bright red circles of temptation. Bob licked his lips. And then his chin and the tip of his nose. Suddenly the past-her-prime hippie belched out loud and smiled, proud of her breaking of accepted social mores. The magic moment broken, Bob staggered away.

No cab stopped to answer his halitosis-laden hail. He sniffed the air. A smile grew, but was never completed the growing cycle. The source, a refrigerated meat truck, passed by. He reached out like a child watching a passing ice cream vendor. Its oversized tires trounced a large puddle and sent a frigid shower of dirty water down his shirt and straight into the poo poo undies.

Bob felt another mighty sneeze coming on. He grabbed for his handkerchief, but too late. A blast of nasal goo splattered the concrete, coalescing into a mobile wad floating on the thin coat of rainwater staining the sidewalk. He watched as it edged past a large rat that was threatening a baby pigeon trapped at the corner of a building. Like its motion picture namesake, the blob changed directions and quickly covered the furry beast with a coat of nasty colors. As its nemesis quick dissolved faster than Speedy Alka-Seltzer the pigeon flew away without so much as a chirp of thanks to its dark savior.

"Ingrate." Bob pressed on through the dark streets, hungry and in need of a hot blooded meal.

The slushing swish of a cab pulling to a sloppy stop across the street caught his attention, its destination a homey lodging called Granny's Bed, Breakfast & Brew. The passenger stepped out. A young woman ran to the door and skidded under the awning. She pulled the hood down from her red cloak and entered the building.

Bob floated into the shadows. "Guess I'll begin the evening with a little tart."

Her name was Cindy and her small apartment reflected the image of a young woman

living contentedly on her own. It was tidy, uncoordinated and filled with bric-a-brac,

odds and ends, and inexpensively framed prints of small animals with large sad eyes and

heart-melting smiles. Pastel colors dominated with pink being her favorite. Her bookshelf contained a few old college textbooks and a lot of paperback romances. Stuffed animals of all sizes and varieties were scattered around the living room. The place was "cute." The first time the building's maintenance man went in he shrieked.

– Excerpt from ***Vampire Bimbo's ...on Spring Break***

Caldera III – A Man of Blood

~~Excerpt~~

Prologue

The witch stirred her bubbling vat of pinto beans with the working end of a walking stick. Nearby, on a cracked slab of old planking, flies circled a short stack of warm tortillas. Caldera tried to sit up, but he only had the strength to rest on his elbows and stare at the old hag. She looked more like a gnarled cottonwood worn gray by wind and water than a human being. He grunted in pain. Belle McKenzie's poison enflamed his arteries and veins and every breath seared his insides with agony. The gashes across his belly where she had raked him with the broken bottle of poison dripped blood onto the old woman's porch. She laughed – a coarse and sadistic sound.

"Time to make choice, young Caldera."

He coughed as he spoke. "Where am I?"

"Hell."

He coughed again and wiped blood on his sleeve. "The hell it is, old woman. This is your house in Privy."

"Same thing."

He struggled more, but found only the strength to sit up with his back resting against a strong sapling hacked down and used to support the flimsy, brush roof over the witch's porch. The smell of pintos was strong. He was hungry and as he rubbed his belly he discovered that his gut wounds had healed.

"I'm dreaming, ain't I?"

"You're in the middle ground."

"Seems to be the way of things."

She stirred again. Whiffs of steam swirled from the pot and floated around the stringy gray hair. Her head looked like some long dead animal trapped and hanging in a tree after a flash flood. "Middle ground, Caldera. You must choose now the road of your future."

"A man ain't got no choice 'bout his future, old woman."

"You're not like other men. You choose. I help you." The wrinkled lines in her face squeezed into a horizontal position. No one other than the witch would have called that movement a smile.

The flames scouring Caldera's insides cooled down and floated away like a mist caught by the morning sun. His pain was gone. "I am dreaming. But I remember you. When me 'n Benny came to collect your taxes—"

"I made you a promise then, didn't I?"

"Yeah. I remember that, too."

"What did I promise you?"

"Pain."

"My promise true?"

"Yeah, kept your damn promise. Pain for everybody I ever cared about. You didn't say nothing about that."

"Then you know my words are true."

"Yeah."

"You believe?"

"Yeah."

"Say it!"

"Damn it, I believe."

"Good. Now I help with your future?"

"Just how the hell are you gonna do that, old woman?"

She stirred the pintos and raked the walking stick across the bottom of the vat to loosen those that had burned and stuck. She bent over face down into the steam and breathed deeply. "I give you choice, young Caldera."

He rubbed his belly again and breathed in the rich, earthy smell. "I ain't all that young."

"All the world is young to me. You make choice. Now."

"What choice, witch?"

"Famous choice. Caldera can live a long life, good life, but nobody will ever know his name."

"Or? There's always a damn 'or.'"

"Or Caldera can be famous, maybe even a...what's the word...hero." Her face crinkled again. She apparently liked what was coming next. "But you die young. Soon I think."

"I am dreaming."

"Choose your future, Caldera. What do you want!"

Caldera stood up, his strength fully returned, and walked over to the witch. He looked her straight in the eyes. "I want me a plate of beans."

– Excerpt from **_Caldera III – A Man of Blood_**

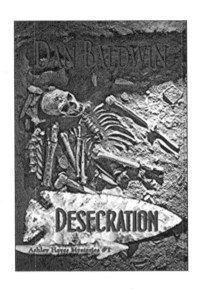

Desecration

~~Excerpt~~

Chapter One

"Dem bones, dem bones, dem... dry bones?" *Naw, that's not it.* The man with the red-line eyes wiped a bit of drool from the corner of his mouth. "Foot bone connected to the leg bone. Leg bone connected to the knee bone." *No. There were more bones, lots of bones, lots and lots of bones.* He scratched his left wrist as if trying to dig out the answer from his flesh.

"Dry bones? Bone dry? Bonehead? Boner?" The words banged around the inside of his skull like a handful of pebbles rattling in the skin of an old, dried up gourd. They shattered and splintered into sharp, ragged pieces that punched tiny holes into his brain, holes that itched like the mosquito bites folks get back in the deep swamps. He desperately wanted to claw the inside of his head. He was a scrawny, dried out stinkweed of a man with a sad face that could easily morph itself into the warm glow of sincerity when bumming a smoke, a ride or a hump out in the parking lot. That same face could just as easily twist into an ugly, profane snarl spitting out the devil's own curses upon hearing the inevitable "No," "Sorry," or "Get the hell out of my face!"

His name was Clovis Bassett and he was searching for the string. The thing was wound up somewhere inside him, deep beneath the dirty skin. *The skin.* He never thought of his body as his own. It was always *the* head, *the* foot, *the* gut, *the* string. By his fiftieth year, he'd pretty much figured out that the string was located somewhere down deep in his left arm, maybe hidden deep within the bones. *Dem bones.* He would find it soon. He had to. And then he'd give it a pull, just a slow and gentle tug. The pain would be exquisite, a foreshadowing of the agonizing bliss to follow. He could almost see it happening. First the skin would rip open, neatly, like the shelling of a purple hull pea. Pull the string up the spine of the pea and *pop*. The rich insides would be exposed: muscle, tissue, and blood. *The blood.* He wondered which would be more satisfying: watching the exposed tissues pumping, flexing and bleeding, or the actual slow, lip-biting rip through the leathery, spotted, old skin?

First, he had to find and mark it so he'd never lose it again, so when the time was finally right he could give it that one final tug. *How? Bone black. That's it! Bone black.* That's how the ancient, wise ones did it. Burn some bones to charcoal. Burn 'em to filthy ashes. White to black. Add a little grease and you had the first Magic Marker. Then find that damn string and let X mark the spot. It would not escape him again. He pulled his thin fingers from the sides of his head and looked up. *Where am I? How did I get here?*

He had stumbled into the Tall Pines Restaurant and Lounge at Murfreesboro, south-central Arkansas. It was a big, warm, wide-open place where a waitress's friendly "Hi" and country music was as much a part of the atmosphere as the bacon grease floating on the haze of cigarette smoke that passed for air. Huge beams, left rough-cut for effect, supported a high, vaulted ceiling. The equally rough and unpainted plank walls were dented at precisely the same level by generations of overweight pulpwood haulers who couldn't sit without leaning back in their metal chairs.

The number of customers had dropped considerably between breakfast and lunch and Bassett tried to ignore the only other diners, two portly survivors of the local timber industry. Their laughter sent a shock of anger through his system and he fired a dangerous scowl back across the room. It was an automatic movement that achieved an instant reaction. The two old men began studying their plates. Something in the thin stranger's eyes raised the hairs on the back of their necks. The effect was like hearing the are-you-sure-you-want-to-step-here buzz of a rattlesnake down in the tall grass.

"Who does that sumbitch think he is?"

"Let it be."

"Sumbitch."

They went back to their morning coffee and continued trading off-color jokes with Jan, the regular day waitress. She was in her fifties, thin, and retaining just enough veneer of her former glory as a high school beauty queen. She was friendly and had an ageless smile that could make some of the good deacons "wonder if," and at the same time invite their plump, patient and big-haired wives in on the joke. The food at Tall Pines was good and there were always large portions splayed on its thick, well-worn white plates, but it was Jan and her smile who kept the regulars coming back.

Bassett ignored the men and rubbed his arm.

One of the retired men shook off the hostility he felt for the dirty man across the room by changing the subject. With great and exaggerated dignity, as Jan watched, he dragged his last half-biscuit slowly and elegantly across the plate, a small craft easing through a sea of butter and syrup, grease and gravy. "If the surup' tears it in half, that means they got Mama cookin' back there in the kitchen," he said. He looked his companion of many years directly in the eye. With the conviction of a newly converted Christian making his first witness to his fellow sinners, he said, "Real or store-bought, it's the only way to tell."

Across the table, his good friend wiped his mouth and blew his nose on a napkin, rolled the paper into a tight ball and tossed it into the leftover grits and goo on his plate. "Some folks might just take a bite out of it and chew." The comment was dutifully ignored.

The lonely biscuit ended its journey unscathed and intact. The pilot, shaking his head in remorse, held it above his plate. "I've patched flat tires with these things."

Jan slapped him gently on his shoulder and left the table in amused protest. She glanced around the room looking for tip material. *The pickins' are lean, downright skinny.*

Bassett didn't notice her until she was standing over him. He quickly clamped his right hand around his left wrist, as if protecting some personal treasure or hiding some dark shame. The inside of his head began to itch even more fiercely.

She flashed her best smile. "Refill, Hon?"

Like an old cat, he shook his head from side to side and began trembling. Tiny sweat beads popped out on his dirty forehead as he tried to make out what she was saying. A soft, terrible fluttering inside his head kept slapping her words around, scattering them in directions he could not follow. It sounded as if he were inside a muffled bass drum surrounded by a hundred more, all lightly pounding different rhythms. No," he grunted, barely hearing his own answer. He grabbed his cup with a shaky hand and took a sip of the cold coffee, a dismissal.

The old men were standing beside the cash register. One of them shouted, "Jan, breakfast on the house today?"

She glanced at Bassett. "I'll be right back." She left to take their money.

The men enjoyed a final, just-barely dirty joke.

Jan pretended to be offended and spiked the light green ticket on a spindle.

The men left with a wave, a grin and enough dirty thoughts to get them through the morning. Jan grabbed the coffee pot and returned to her hostile customer. "You okay, Hon? You need an aspirin or something?" She refilled his cup automatically.

He was still trembling, still rubbing his left arm near the wrist. "No. It's that picture on the wall."

Jan forced a smile. *Strange bird.* But they often got a lot of backwoods boys dropping into the restaurant. Too many cousins marrying cousins back there in the lonely hollows. Some of them were hard to look at.

Bassett's face twitched and his eyes blinked erratically. He made a weak gesture toward the walls. They were decorated with prints of old circus posters, Native American arrowheads mounted in gray shadow boxes, and artwork by local talent clearly destined for careers in fast food, homemaking, and gas station management. Each frame and box had a small, circular price tag licked and affixed to a bottom corner, each little spot yellowed and curled with ancient humidity. Bassett tried again, pointed to a paint-by-the-numbers version of a famous bit of western art. It featured a lone Indian on horseback, his spear dropping to the dust as he entered the sunset, his back bent by defeat and despair.

"It's called 'End of the Trail,' I think," Jan said. "Priced right." She flashed the smile, but her customer wasn't buying.

"Naw," he mumbled.

"How about some breakfast or a Honey Bun?"

"I ain't feeling too good, Lady." It was a threat and an invitation to leave him alone. He gripped his cup with shaking hands, spilling coffee on the red and white plastic table cloth.

She held her smile, but with obvious effort. "Don't worry about that, I change 'em after breakfast anyway." Bassett grunted something unintelligible and Jan glanced around. They were alone in the dining room and the kitchen help was way the hell out of sight. She gripped the coffee pot tightly, her subconscious mind reacting to something her conscious mind did not yet recognize.

Bassett nodded upwards. "That picture up there bothers me. I'm a' Indian."

She brightened and loosened her grip. "Really?"

"Caddo... Caddo Indian."

"Well, we're probably cousins or somethin'," Jan said. "I'm Indian on my daddy's side. Apache, I think."

Bassett knocked over his cup. It fell to the concrete floor and shattered. Jan immediately pulled a handful of paper napkins from the rusted metal container. She squatted down with a polite grunt and stemmed the small, dark tide. "Happens all the time, Hon. I'll clean it up and get you another."

The thin, ugly little man watched her walk back behind the counter where she picked up a whisk broom and a dust pan. His eyes followed her every step. *Apache! Enemy of my people!* Hate touched him, a tide of overwhelming, thought-numbing emotion. It was at that moment of purest evil that his boney fingers found the string. There, right in the middle of his left wrist. *The wrist.* He gave it a quick, tentative tug. The string ripped a thin, neat line about a quarter of an inch up his arm. The pain was brief and searing, but he could see no blood.

Jan returned to the damnedest sight she'd encountered in years: a grown man shedding tears in public over a spilled cup of coffee. For some reason he was pinching his wrist. *What next?* "It's okay, Hon." She placed a hand on his shoulder and every silent alarm carried by every woman in the history of the world went into scream mode. The message from her subconscious mind finally showed up in her conscious mind: *Run!* The warning was far too late.

Clovis Bassett moved so swiftly that Jan never knew what killed her: the blade of a pocket knife rammed under her rib cage directly into her heart. Her eyes grew wide in shock and terror. Bassett rammed the knife in and out a few times and then shoved her head back with such force that the crack of her neck sounded like the snap of brittle fire wood on a cold Arkansas morning. As she fell away, he pulled the blade from her body. He shouted and screamed in victory and vengeance, but heard nothing except the fluttering drums inside his head.

The scream brought an old black woman, the cook, from the kitchen. She was as large as a professional mezzo-soprano and her scream was just as loud. Her shrieking joined the killer's in a duet of terror. Her hands slapped uselessly at the counter in true, Deep South Christian horror as Bassett turned Jan over, grabbed her short blond hair, and pulled her head from the floor, the bloody knife still in his other hand. Horror turned to hysteria and the black woman started shoving plates, cups, silverware, anything, everything off the counter. She crashed and pushed her way down its entire length. It ended near the front door. "Merciful Father! Merciful Father! Merciful Father!" The last item she shoved to the floor was a rack of tourist brochures advertising the nearby Caddo Experience Village and Museum.

– Excerpt from **Desecration**

Dank Summit & Other Stories

~~Excerpt~~

"No More White Guilt"

Oscar Wilwhite was in an anxious hurry as he taped up the huge, hand-lettered sign in the big picture window facing the street. His eyes were fixed not on the signs or his store, but on the Andy's Handy Dandy store down the street. Wilwhite's We Got It All StoreMart was in a price war with the Dandy. So far, he had been winning, although at the price of severely reduced profit margins. The hand-made signs across his storefront advertising slashed prices had brought in the customers and those customers had been buying. Today, Saturday, would or at least should be his biggest day. He rushed inside and prepared his excuses for the sold-out items, practiced his best bait-n-switcheroo lines and prepared a stack of his "Back At 'Cha" rain checks.

Mrs. Wilhite, Dora Mae, would be coming in to help with the afternoon rush, but until then the duty fell on Oscar and his nephew, Algonquin. Al wasn't all that swift and Oscar claimed that the young man was more than a few gallons short of a full tank. But, he was a moderately hard worker and it was his skilled penmanship that had created the sign that now dominated the front window.

"Think you got enough signs up there, Uncle Oscar?"

"Nothing attracts a crowd like bright ink on white butcher paper, Al."

"Can I ding the door now?"

Oscar nodded and Al jumped into action.

The StoreMart was an old wooden building, a converted warehouse for the now defunct Dank Summit Feed & Grain Store. A large wooden porch, shaded by the tin roof, wrapped around the front and half both sides of the building. The porch served as a waiting room, community hall and betting parlor for the men waiting on the womenfolk to do their weekly shopping. All week it had also served as a gallery for Al's hand-lettered artwork, which promoted everything from bacon and bedding to clothing and clawhammers. The young man jumped to the front double door. A bell over the left door dinged as he opened and locked the door in place.

"Okay, Al. Now, go stack up a bunch of them Vi-enny sausage cans in aisle three next to the crackers. Then put up them oil cans over in automotive."

Al nodded and rushed off.

After he was gone, Oscar said, "That boy couldn't find a basketball in number three washtub."

Screeching tires on the street and a loud "What the..." drew his attention to Rev. E.A. Tinsdale, who had just brought his church's Cadillac SUV to a halt. Tinsdale led the small community of Dank Summit's largest black church. A reformed, musician who had toured the Dixie circuit, he played a mean saxophone and every year he led a "Sax 'n Salvation" crusade around the local churches. He stared out at the StoreMart and looked over to Oscar. "Are you crazy, man!"

Oscar waved, a confused look on his face.

Rev. Tinsdale shook his head. "I'll be back. I'm putting the word out on you. I'll be back." He drove off faster than the Israelites fleeing Pharaoh's chariots.

Oscar wandered back into his store where he discovered Al stacking Vienna Sausage cans in a neat pyramid on aisle five right next to the anti-acids. "Dagnabbit, Al!"

"Whut?"

"I said aisle three."

"I thought you was joking. You ever ate a bunch of these things? I once had the slobbers for nigh un to—"

"Never mind. Rev. Tinsdale's coming by later. He'll probably be loading up for a Sunday all day picnic on the ground or some such. Start sweeping down these aisles."

"Yes, sir."

"The floors, Al. Just the floors."

"Gotcha."

Oscar slowly marched up and down each aisle – bedding, hardware, housewares, cosmetics, medicinal, food and beverage. All was in readiness for another successful day – all save his "Vi-enny" sausages. Customers filtered in – not many, but the day was young and Oscar knew things would pick up. He was moving the sausage cans over to the food aisle when he noticed a commotion out front. He walked over to the front door. Across the street half a dozen or so young people were chanting a call and response led by the town's throwback to the sixties, Jimi Strawberry.

"The whole world is watching," Jimi shouted.

"The whole world is watching," his merry band responded.

Oscar scratched his head. "Watching what?" He stepped out on the porch and looked around, even up to the sky. Nothing.

Jimi Strawberry saw him and pointed a liver-spotted hand his way. "End apartheid now!

"In apartments now!"

"Jimi looked over his group and shouted, *"Apartheid*!"

"Apartheid now!"

"No," Jimi shouted. "*End* Apartheid now."

"End Apartments now!"

Oscar sighed and went back inside. A few moments later the sound of women's voices accompanied by a saxophone brought him back. Tinsdale was leading more than a dozen or so of the women's church chorus in *God Will Take Care of You*. The way Tinsdale the women pointed at Oscar's store indicated "take care of you" was more of a curse than a blessing. Jimi Strawberry's merry band slowly edged over to join the choir. They didn't know the words, but they knew how to point.

– Excerpt from **Dank Summit & Other Stories**

Made in the USA
Middletown, DE
29 October 2023

41492612R00096